A CHURCHGOING WOMAN

ROXANA NASTASE

Scarlet Leaf

2019

ISBN: 9781386139805

PUBLISHED BY SCARLET LEAF
Toronto, Canada

To Raluca and Vicentiu

For their constant support and friendship

TABLE OF CONTENTS

CHAPTER I – JUST ANOTHER DAY IN CHURCH

"Oh, not again," Emily Logan muttered to herself, and irritated, brushed a strand of blond hair off her face.

She glanced at the minister. He was droning on and on about one sin or another. Ashamed, Emily admitted that she had lost track of the service.

Emily pushed hard on the armrests of her chair. She stood up and staggered for a moment, which made her wince.

Emily had to go to the restroom, again, and fast. Well, as fast as she could. These days, it felt like the baby danced on her bladder with a vengeance.

Emily turned to move up the aisle and met Lorna Carter's scornful eyes. Lorna smirked and then turned to the woman next to her, whispering and shaking her head.

Emily knew the rumors Lorna had spread about her for over half a year now, but she didn't have the strength to deal with that right then.

Eight months ago, someone attacked Emily on her way back home. She was struck from behind and lost consciousness. When she came to, she found that the man had dragged her into an alley behind a closed shop. Her dress was in rags, and a huge man loomed over her. She struggled, but he struck her savagely until she lost consciousness again.

The man raped Emily that night. She had just turned sixteen.

A police car found her only in the wee hours of the morning, and they drove Emily to the catholic hospital of the county. There, the doctor took a rape kit, but the police lost it soon afterward, so they couldn't make an arrest.

Fearing the consequences of the rape, Emily's mother had asked the doctor to give the emergency contraception pill to her daughter, but he refused her. He told her that they might find a hospital or a clinic willing to do that in one of the surrounding counties.

Her mother took Emily there when the doctor discharged her from the hospital, but it was already too late. A month later, they found out that the girl was pregnant with her rapist's child.

The news overwhelmed the young woman, and for over two months, her mother watched her steadily, afraid that Emily would harm herself. After those two months, Emily returned to something close to normal.

When she finally stepped out of the house and went back to school, she heard the horrible rumors lurking around. People were saying that she only got what she had asked.

Emily had been afraid that people would look at her and see a victim. Now, she knew better. They looked at her and saw a whore.

Soon enough, she found out who was behind the ugly rumors: the churchgoing Lorna Carter. She belittled everyone and bullied at least three parts of the town. If Lorna decreed that people shouldn't talk to someone, most of the town people listened to her because they were afraid of her.

Emily learned to deal with that, too. Anyway, some people still visited her and tried to support her.

Emily passed by Lorna's pew and ignored her. That made Lorna's blood boil. She considered that no one should trifle with her, so she had to teach that little scamp a lesson.

Lorna followed Emily's trip to the door with narrowed eyes. Then she turned to her old friend, Annaliese, to plot Emily's total social demise. She still had a few cards left up to her sleeve, and she couldn't wait for the day when she would crush that white trash under her heel.

Emily still had some way to go to the door. Lorna's eyes bored holes in her back.

The young woman passed by John Rand, and he smiled at her. Then the man gazed at Lorna Carter beyond Emily. The hatred in his hard black eyes startled Lorna for a second, but then, an ugly smile flourished on her thin lips.

John Rand had worked in the bakery on Main Street until Lorna bullied Jeremiah, the owner, and he had fired Rand, with no reference. Rand couldn't find another job in that town or the next one, and he also had an old mother to support. Lorna didn't care. The man reaped what he sowed.

With indifference, Lorna's eyes moved back to Emily, whose gait reminded her of a duck. Lorna's ugly grin widened.

Emily still had about twelve feet to the door. She stumbled, and Aileen Edwards grasped her arm and helped her recover her balance.

Aileen shook her head with sadness over the seventeen-year-old girl's state. Then, her blue eyes threw darts toward Lorna Carter. Lorna scowled back.

Aileen had also gotten what she merited. She had dared to contradict Lorna before the church committee. Lorna couldn't forget or forgive, so she had taken care of Aileen's marriage.

Lorna's eyes shone with disdain and then moved back to Emily. Eight more feet to the door. Lorna wouldn't have been sorry to see the teenager stumble again.

Emily passed by a family of five, and the children smiled at her. Lorna's eyes narrowed to slits. The mother immediately called the children to order.

On the other side of the aisle, Matthew Jackson witnessed the look exchange and molted rage shone in his black eyes. He fixated on Lorna, but she merely smirked at him and shrugged. He was unimportant, only a bug, so Lorna didn't worry about him. Her eyes went back to Emily. Now, she passed by Lorna's son, Edward. With a sad smile, Edward tried to assist Emily, but she rejected him. Lorna's face contorted into a mask of fury. That stupid pup! He still sighed after that girl.

Dan Hanson opened the door for Emily and whispered something in her ear. She shook her head but softened the rejection by stroking the older man's arm. Hanson smiled at her lowered head and closed the door behind her.

Then, he turned back to face the altar. His eyes intersected Lorna's. He growled. If eyes could kill, Lorna would have been murdered where she stood.

CHAPTER 2 – LIFE AND DEATH ON SUNDAY EVENING

When the piercing pain came, Emily dropped the basket with the tomatoes she had just gathered and groaned. The stabbing pain in her back intensified and brought tears in her eyes. The young girl doubled over.

She had been having pains now and then since noon. Emily had thought that the weight of the baby caused the sharp pains in her lower back, so she tried not to pay attention to them.

Her eyes widened in alarm when water pooled at her feet suddenly. She was in labor, and that scared her. Emily was alone at home. Her mother worked the afternoon shift at the factory in the next town, and Emily knew she wouldn't come back home before ten.

Emily knew that she couldn't call the hospital, and that panicked her more. They had had the phone disconnected two days ago, and they hadn't had the money to pay the bill yet. Her mother's paycheck was due only in three days.

Anyway, it didn't matter because she couldn't have called an ambulance. Her medical insurance barely covered the birth, and that only if there weren't any complications.

Emily looked in the distance, but there wasn't anyone in sight. They lived beyond the edge of town, and their closest neighbor was a mile and a half down the road. She didn't even know if the neighbors would be willing to help. They had avoided her lately, but Emily couldn't condemn them. They needed to take care of themselves and couldn't cross Lorna Carter.

On the other hand, if I crossed the field behind the house, I'd reach the road to the hospital, she thought. There were only about three and a half miles to walk, and maybe, a car would pass by and give her a lift.

Once she made her decision, Emily went inside the house and forgot about the tomatoes spread in the grass.

The clock chimed. It was only nine o'clock.

Emily would have liked to shower and change before going to the hospital, but she could barely stand. So, she picked up her bag with documents and left. Emily was ashamed to get to the hospital like that. However, if she had tried to shower, she might not have been able to leave at all, and she was far too scared to remain in the house.

She wobbled out of the house and down the stairs at the back of the house. Her back ached, but she started to cross the field with determination. It stretched far under her frightened eyes.

What if I don't make it? Emily wondered, but then she shook her head. *I have to do it.*

She hung the strap of the handbag on one shoulder. Her right hand clutched on her lower back, Emily started her trip to the hospital, and then she trudged ahead.

Pains came and went, taking her breath away, and Emily would bend over whenever her abdomen contracted. Every pain left her breathless for a minute or so and made her walk with more difficulty.

Twenty minutes later, a powerful pain gripped her, and Emily cried out. With the pain, the urge to push came, as well. Emily fell on the ground with a terrified shout. She tried to stop pushing but to no avail.

With shaking hands, she took off her underwear. The contractions were close now. They melted into a big one, and Emily couldn't catch her breath anymore. She began panting, and tears trailed down her cheeks. Her body took over, and she felt the baby coming. Emily clenched her fists hard, and her knuckles turned white.

Then, the aching wave stopped for a few seconds. Emily tried to breathe normally, but a new contraction seized her, and with an inhuman cry, she pushed again and felt the baby sliding out on the ground.

It was 9:25 on November 6th, 2016, Sunday evening.

***

The Carters' house was on the other end of the town, in a square that included only five streets. That was the fashionable part, inhabited by rich people, who thought that they were the pillars of the community. They looked down their nose to the mere mortals, who lived beyond the border of that square.

The commercial street separated the square from the unfashionable part of town. Here, in that square, the houses were old but kept with care. Lawns were perfectly manicured, and drives sported the latest model in cars. Flowers bordered the front walls, and flimsy curtains adorned the windows.

The Carters' house was a two-story, red brick, erected on the corner of Orchids Street. Three tall oaks shadowed the windows on one side of the lawn. On the other, a statue of Madonna overlooked a small garden.

At 9:20, on November 6, 2016, the house was almost dark. Only the kitchen window glimmered in the light of the ceiling lamp.

Silence surrounded the area. At 9:25, a brief cry erupted from the back of the Carters' house. The sound of the war movie on TV from their neighbors' living room swallowed it.

In her once immaculate kitchen, Lorna Carter lay on the floor, stabbed five times in her chest, and once in her abdomen in rapid succession. Her blood spilled on the well-scrubbed floor.

She had cried out when her gaze fell on the knife pushed down to her chest, but after the first blow in her chest, Lorna couldn't do anything but gurgle. The knife penetrated her chest the third time. Her life left the body, and her eyes became glassy.

***

At a quarter to ten, Dan Hanson knocked on the Logans' door. He knew that Margaret Logan was supposed to come from work at around that time.

He had come to bring some apples and pears from his garden to Margaret and Emily. Dan Hanson nurtured several fruit-trees and was very generous with the fruit he gathered. The man thought mostly of Emily. The girl reminded him of his daughter, and he couldn't look upon her without tenderness.

Dan knocked on the door again, but no one answered. He called out, "Emily, Margaret? Are you there, in the back? It's me, Dan."

No answer came, so he went around the house to the garden. Dan was sure that he would find Emily there. The garden had become her oasis of peace for the last few months.

Dan reached the garden and suddenly stopped. His eyes fell on the tomatoes scattered on the ground, and the pool of water Emily had left behind. Dan needed a moment, but he understood what had happened soon enough. Yet, he still called once more, "Emily? Are you all right, girl?"

His question met with silence. The man went to the back door, which was open, and peered inside. He noticed Emily's handbag wasn't where she used to leave it. He must have seen that bag on that corner table a hundred times.

Dan scratched his head, trying to bring light over the situation. He knew that Margaret couldn't have come in time to drive Emily to the hospital, and Emily didn't have a car. The Logans didn't afford too many luxuries, and a second car was a luxury. He also knew that their phone wasn't working. He had tried to call before coming to visit, but the robot informed him about the suspension of the service.

He didn't think that Emily had gone to any of their neighbors. They hadn't been in close relations with them lately, and most of them, if not all, were afraid of that woman, Carter. They wouldn't have helped Emily.

Dan looked out of the back door suddenly. There was only one possibility left. Emily had decided to go to the hospital on foot. His best guess was that she had probably thought of crossing the field to reach the road.

He didn't waste time but broke into a run. Despite his age, Dan was still agile and in good physical shape. He still farmed by himself, and farming was back-breaking work.

Dan ran down the stairs and then across the field. He didn't stop until he had heard the whimpering of a child.

Somewhat less worried, Dan started looking for Emily. He found her lying on the ground, drenched in sweat, her eyes closed, and strain lines in the corner of her mouth and eyes. His heart ached for her. He had seen his wife giving birth, and that event had marked him for a long time.

Dan looked over Emily attentively and noticed that she had wiped the child with her underwear and taken the baby in her arms. Of course, the baby still had the umbilical cord attached, and Dan didn't know if that was good or bad.

The man hunched near Emily. He stroked her face with his roughened hand. "Emily... Emily, wake up," Dan insisted when it became clear that she wasn't aware of his presence.

Emily's lashes fluttered, and her tired eyes laid on him.

"Mr. Hanson," Emily murmured when she recognized the blurry figure.

"Yes, muffin. It's me," Dan said. He smiled at her and brushed her drenched blond hair off her face. Then he explained to her, "I will take you up in my arms, Emily, and carry you to my car. We have to go to the hospital, all right? Can you hold onto the baby?" Dan asked Emily and then stroked the side of her face encouragingly.

She tried to answer but couldn't. Her mouth and throat were parched. Her lips felt dry, and she had the skin in the corner of her mouth cracked. Emily realized that she couldn't utter a sound, so she only nodded.

Dan panted a little and staggered under her weight, but he managed to rise with her in his arms. Then, he started back to the car he had left in the Logans' drive. His stride was long, even though labored. He needed to take the two to the hospital and with maximum haste.

***

Gus Carter came back home at 9:45. He got off his car with some difficulty and puffed like a whale. He didn't move with the same agility he used to have a few decades ago. His protruding belly hampered him most of the time, but Gus had learned to live with it.

Gus wouldn't have liked to give up his beer and steaks, and unfortunately, the doctor had prescribed precisely that. That, and some exercising. As if he started exercising so late in life when he hadn't done it in his youth! *Huh!*

Gus fumed and craved for an argument. Lorna had told Gus that his friend, the mayor, had called and asked that Gus would come to his home at once. Gus went there, but the housekeeper had told him that his friend had taken his family to have dinner in town. Gus had cursed all the way home.

The mayor, Stewart Black, lived in a ranch outside the town line, and the drive to his house had taken almost half an hour. The days when Gus drove fast for the sake of driving were long gone. Then, he could have made that trip in half the time. Now, he never crossed over 30-40 miles an hour, so he drove half an hour one way and another back.

That was how Gus had lost an hour on a Sunday evening. He could have watched the film on TV or, better yet, a football match if that witch had allowed it.

Gus had wondered, and more than once, who wore the trousers in the house. He had never liked the answer.

He couldn't wait to see Lorna and tell her to clean her ears. God knew who had called and asked for him. Not that it mattered, anyway. He wouldn't go out again for anything in the whole world. Monday was just around the corner, and a man needed a day of rest. He slaved enough during the week.

Gus slammed the front door with fury and shouted, "Lorna, where the heck are you, woman? You sent me on a wild goose chase, and I wasted my entire Sunday because of you. Come here, Lorna. I want to talk to you." *Damn your hide, woman.*

Lorna didn't answer, and Gus muttered under his breath. *Too bossy by half. And she thinks she can ignore me. Huh! Damn the old bat.*

That woman drove him mad, and he swore that one of these days, he would make her pay. *Damn, interfering woman, blabbering all day long! She takes the joy out of a man's life,* Gus mumbled to himself.

Life with Lorna had always been a trial. She had tricked him good, and he had to marry her.

Gus thought of his marital life as his penance for every sin he had ever committed. Surely, he would go to heavens when he died. The woman was mean and petty, and his life had gone from bad to worse during the last few years.

He stomped to the kitchen, his chest heaving. The light beaconed him, and he was puffing under the steam of his anger. He had worked himself into a leather.

"Lorna," he shouted again when he entered the kitchen, but anything else he wanted to say froze in his throat.

Lorna's body, soaked in blood, looked like a pincushion. Gus lost his dinner promptly, and then, he didn't know how to get out of the kitchen faster and call the sheriff.

CHAPTER 3 – A DISPATCHER WITH A SPECIAL SENSE OF HUMOR

Bored out of her mind, Norma Jean was merely filing her fingernails when the phone rang. She threw her fiery hair over her left shoulder and scowled.

Then Norma Jean admired her long fingernails and thought to let the phone ring. She wasn't in the mood to take any calls that night, and she didn't care if half the county was out for a kill.

"Aren't you going to take that?" Deputy Henderson asked from the door, dusting off his hat.

Norma Jean glanced at the tall figure looming in the door, and her scowl deepened. She hadn't heard the deputy coming back from his round, although he wasn't such a small man. He was well over 6.2, in her opinion. Now, she had to answer the damn phone.

She waved her hand in the deputy's direction to shut him up and picked up the receiver with a grim expression in her green eyes. The deputy pitied the person who thought to call at that hour.

"The Sherriff's Office," she mumbled and then listened to the frantic voice at the other end of the line. Muffled bits and pieces of words reached the deputy's ear, but he couldn't understand their meaning.

"And who did you say you were?" Norma Jean asked rudely, and the deputy shook his head in desperation.

He knew why Norma Jean worked there. It wasn't because of her secretarial skills or polite phone attitude, but because she was the sheriff's sister-in-law. That was how she had landed the job.

Of course, no one else would have hired her. Before working for the Sheriff's Office, she had made the tour of all businesses in the county, or so people said.

It was common knowledge she couldn't hold a job for more than a mere three days anywhere else. She had been fired more often than some people changed their shirt.

There, in the sheriff's office, her brother-in-law closed his eyes to her unorthodox manners, and no one wondered he had lost or misplaced all the complaints filed against Norma Jean. And there had been quite a few. Chris Henderson had even witnessed a few of the accusations.

A while back, the deputy had wondered why the sheriff didn't worry about not being elected again. His behavior towards the constituents and his support for Norma Jean were telling.

Anyway, Chris found out why less than a year ago, when the rape kit related to Emily Logan's rape was misplaced. Of course, after being lost for a while, the collection became useless, and they never resolved the case. Then Henderson put two and two together: the private discussions the sheriff had with Lorna Carter and Sheriff Willow's confidence in the future election. The young man had been agonizing over Logan's case ever since. He'd wanted to do something but didn't have a clue what he could do.

"Aha...aha... I'd say to ease down on the booze and go to bed," Norma Jean's voice boomed, followed by the receiver slamming in the hook.

Deputy Henderson winced and watched her with wide eyes. He'd seen and heard her doing a lot of things but, until then, she'd never treated someone with so much contempt.

"Who was on the phone?" Henderson asked and put the hat on the top of his desk.

Norma Jean only waved her hand as if she were sick and tired with the subject. Henderson insisted in a steely voice, though, "Who was on the darn phone?"

Norma Jean glanced at Chris as though she saw him for the first time. Her eyes swept over his thick, black and unruly hair, dark blue eyes, the expanse of his chest, and muscular thighs, and her heart did a little tumble. Henderson was a tall and strong man, but he used to be an easy-going fellow. His present voice and demeanor were out of the ordinary, and something stirred in Norma Jean's heart or maybe somewhere else.

"Just a drunk," she replied briefly and shrugged.

"Exactly who?" Henderson asked again, and his sternness made Norma Jean shiver.

He's like a damn terrier with a bone, she thought, now getting angry.

"Gus Carter," she said through clenched teeth.

Her temper was rising. No one questioned her actions in that office. They all knew who she was, and Norma Jean knew to use the law of the land to her advantage. Henderson might have been a hunk – all right, a sexy hunk, but that didn't give him leeway to treat her that way. She would have to teach him a lesson or two.

"Gus Carter is not a drunk," Henderson observed in the same steely voice, and his eyes turned into slits.

"Everybody is a drunk," the petite curvy woman responded nonchalantly. "Even you can get drunk," Norma Jean remarked, and the light reflected in the green of her eyes when she smirked at him.

"Maybe, but that's neither here nor there. The man doesn't get drunk. Ever," Chris Henderson stressed and cut the air with his palm. "Get it through your thick skull, Norma Jean. He never gets drunk. What did he say, Norma Jean?" he prodded again.

Henderson had a bad feeling. The hair on his forearms was standing up, and something close to anxiety was playing havoc with his heart.

Norma Jean fluttered her hand again, and then, she admitted, "Something about Lorna being on the floor and blood everywhere. No doubt that the man is in his bottles," she remarked. "After a good night of sleep, he'll recover," she observed in her usual sluggish manner.

"Are you out of your mind?" Henderson shouted. "Someone called to announce a murder, and you sent them to bed?" His voice rose more and more with every word, and Norma Jean flinched at every higher sound.

"Don't get your bowels in a knot, Deputy," she tried to hold her own. "The man was drunk, no question about it. I tell you. Nobody would touch Lorna. Believe me. The man or woman who'd dare that isn't born yet," she said, nodding emphatically.

Chris Henderson just shook his head in disbelief. The woman had done a lot of things in that office, but that took the prize.

It was one thing to tell Old Maggie to stuff it when she called about her neighbor's dog, and another to dismiss a murder off-hand just because she wanted to. That was beyond mere negligence and laziness.

"Call the sheriff immediately," he shouted at her with authority. "Tell him to come to Carter's. I'll be there," he added and plucked his hat off his desk. He stormed out of the sheriff's office, grumbling.

"Good riddance," Norma Jean mumbled and picked up her nail filer to resume the grooming of her nails. She admired her long and rounded fingernails and started filing them diligently. She had to start the following week with a flawless manicure.

Ten minutes later, to her dismay, the phone rang again. She glanced at it with a frown but continued filing her nails. She imagined it would stop after ten or so rings. Yet, it didn't.

Annoyed, she snatched the receiver off the hook and shouted irately, "What?"

"Are you out of your mind?" the sheriff's angry reply reached her ears. "Is that how you speak to people?" he bellowed his outrage. "I've just had Gus Carter on the phone. He said that he called to announce that someone had killed Lorna, and you told him to ease off the drink and go to bed. Have you lost your damn senses?" the sheriff roared at the top of his lungs.

With a grimace, Norma Jean moved the receiver away from her ear. She just knew her hearing wouldn't be the same after that conversation. She wondered what got into Kenneth's bonnet.

"Kenneth, listen to me..." she began, trying to soothe him, but he interrupted her immediately in a shout.

"Listen... listen..." he sputtered, unable to find his words for a few moments. "Do you want me to listen to you? You're a crazy broad, Norma Jean, do you know that? You listen here. If Lorna's dead, your job is gone. I don't care what your sister says. You're history," he shouted in an increased volume.

Norma Jean pouted but didn't give up. "You'll see she's not dead," she reassured him, and her voice reeked with confidence.

"That's what you say," he argued back. "But Gus says differently, and he knows what he's talking about," Kenneth replied with contempt. "Where's Henderson?" he asked.

"He went to the Carters'," she replied in a small voice. Now she was afraid.

"At least one of you has their head well screwed," he replied. "I'm off to the Carters' as well. And you try to be polite on the phone from now on if somebody calls or you'll be out on your ear otherwise. Do you understand, Norma Jean?" Kenneth shouted at her again and then disconnected the call.

Norma Jean's feeling of well-being faded. She glanced at her hands but couldn't find joy in her shiny fingernails either.

She knew Kenneth well. He was a stuffy prick, and if he felt a threat to his position, he would feed her to the wolves.

CHAPTER 4 – GUS CARTER IS DAUNTINGLY SOBER

Chris Henderson drove to the Carters' as fast as he could, without the lights on. He didn't have confirmation of an emergency and couldn't use the lights and siren just on a hunch.

He still reeled over Norma Jean's scornful behavior. Norma Jean had a pretty face, and that went well with her curvy and luscious body, but her sly nature had always driven Chris away. He avoided her whenever he could.

When he turned into the Carters' drive, his headlights passed over Gus Carter's overflowing body. The man hunched on the front steps, his head in his hands, lost in God knew what thoughts.

When the lights brushed over him, Gus lifted his head and glanced at the deputy's car. For a moment, he seemed not to understand why the car was in his drive. He brushed his fingers through his messy hair and stood up like a drunk man.

Henderson caught Gus's wobbling movement, and his eyes turned to slits. He hoped to high heaven that Norma Jean hadn't been right about Gus's state. He knew that he wouldn't hear the end of that, otherwise, and the last thing he wanted was to give more ammunition to that woman.

Gus started down the stairs with hesitant steps. He kept wiping his hands off on his pants. His palms were clammy. His legs felt like jelly, and each step demanded more and more strength from him.

He met the deputy at the bottom of the imposing staircase, lined with geraniums in clay pots, and he tried to smile. The grimace on his lips reminded Chris Henderson of a gargoyle he had once seen in a horror movie.

Henderson shook Gus's hand and regretted it instantly. Disgusted, he tried to wipe it off warily, but it was hard not to be evident.

"Good evening, Gus," he greeted the older man in a gentle voice. "What's going on? I understand that you called the Sheriff's Office," he hinted to the conversation he had heard earlier. Well, at least, Chris had heard Norma Jean's side of the discussion.

"That woman…" Gus started to say and choked. He cleared his throat noisily and tried again, "That woman…." He couldn't push the words past his lips, although his throat was working hard.

"What woman, Gus?" Chris Henderson asked and thought of helping the man sit back down on the steps.

Gus's legs were shaking violently now, and Chris was afraid that the man would collapse. He eyed Gus carefully. He wasn't sure that he would be strong enough to support Gus's mass if it came to that. Henderson wasn't a small man, but Gus had the bulk of an ox.

Gus sat carefully on the bottom step. He seemed somewhat older, and new wrinkles lined his grey face. Taking note of all the visible signs, Chris was sure that something out of the ordinary had happened in the Carters' house. Besides, the deputy hadn't sniffed spirits on the older man.

Gus braced his elbows on his raised knees and glanced up at Chris with weary eyes. His thick lips quivered, and he licked the bottom one nervously.

"That woman, the one in the Sheriff's Office, she told me I was drunk," Gus finally said, and his eyes flashed with just anger, but Chris didn't say anything, although he understood that Gus felt insulted.

Afraid that he might lose his position in the sheriff's office, Chris didn't dare to say something detrimental about Norma Jean. He liked his job, even though he didn't get to do what he had once dreamed. And, besides that, there weren't many available jobs going around, and unemployment didn't hold any attraction for Chris.

"So, you spoke to Norma," Chris said softly. "I know that, Gus. I was in the office when the call came. Why did you call? What happened?"

Gus looked at Chris as if horns sprouted on his forehead, and his eyes betrayed his disbelief. Gus had thought the deputy knew what happened. He had come there, after all.

"Lorna's dead," he replied drily, too tired to go into details again.

"Dead?" the deputy repeated.

"Deader than a doorknob," Gus nodded and licked his lips again.

He needed to drink something. Probably water, but he wouldn't have refused a generous glass of bourbon. He shook his head with regret. *I should have thought about it earlier. With this kid here, I can't touch my stash. What if he asks for some?*

Unconsciously, he wiped off his palms on his knees again. Sweat beaded his forehead as well.

"Where is she?" Chris asked, bending one knee to see Gus's eyes better.

Gus pointed his head toward the house, "There, in the kitchen. She's on the floor…" His lips trembled, and he shook his head. "There's so much blood…" A new wave of nausea raised in his throat, and he pushed it back.

"All right," Chris replied. "Stay here, and I'll go to take a look. The sheriff should arrive soon. I told Norma Jean to call him," he threw over his shoulder before starting up the stairs.

Gus fluttered his hand and said, "I called him just before you came. I wouldn't let that Norma Jean thwart me like that. I'm better than that," he nodded confidently.

Gus had regained some of his self-assurance. Now, Chris had before his eyes the man aware of his importance in society. Norma Jean had overstepped her boundaries, and Chris knew that Gus would let the matter die. However, the deputy didn't care one way or another. Norma Jean made her bed after all. She could lie in it now.

Chris climbed the stairs and let himself into the house. Gus had left the door wide open in his rush out, and Chris noticed the bloody footprints that Gus had left in the hall. They were leading to the kitchen.

Carefully, the deputy avoided the footprints that ran the length of the hall and went into the kitchen. On his way, he stole a glance here and there. He wasn't curious to see the interior of Gus's house, even if he had never been invited to the house before. He wanted only to make sure that no one else hid inside and to see what possible clues lay in full sight.

The harsh light coming from the ceiling fell on Lorna's body, sprawled in a pool of almost coagulated blood. The woman had dropped on one side of the kitchen table, one leg slightly bent, and one hand clutched to her chest. She was on her back, and the light fell squarely on her face, revealing every single line and flaw. Her expression had frozen in a mask of utter disbelief. Chris reasoned that the killer must have come as a surprise to the woman.

Chris knew that he didn't need to check for a pulse. Gus had been accurate in his evaluation. Lorna was, indeed, deader than a doorknob.

His gaze fell on the remainings of Gus's dinner, and he closed his eyes. Chris left the kitchen, slightly queasy, as well.

He had never seen murder before, and he couldn't recall a crime in the county during his entire lifetime. They dealt with drunken behavior, domestic arguments, and the occasional theft. Nothing in his career had prepared him for that scene, and he doubted that the sheriff was better suited to investigate a murder.

The deputy reached the front door right after he heard the screech of the sheriff's car, braking in the drive. Gus, who was in the same position he had left him, suddenly looked up, just in time to witness the sheriff coming out of his car.

"Henderson, you're here," the sheriff said and braced his hands on his hips. "That's good. Have you found anything?" he asked, and a quiver of hope penetrated his voice.

Henderson guessed that the sheriff would have liked to put the Norma Jean matter to rest, but he couldn't oblige him. *Now, you'll get it, you, big ass bully.* Yet, he kept his satisfaction hidden and reported in an indifferent voice. "Yes, Sheriff, I did. Lorna Carter lies on the floor in the kitchen. Someone stabbed her multiple times. I didn't approach the body, so I can't tell you how many times exactly."

A shadow crossed the sheriff's face, and he bowed his head with a sigh. He felt defeated. He didn't have too much love for Norma Jean. She might have been a very beautiful broad, but she was rude and smug.

Anyway, Norma Jean had sealed her fate now, as well as his. He knew that his marital life would be hell. His wife had a strong family sense and would have his head for not protecting her little sister.

"What are you going to do about that ne'er do good, Norma Jean?" Gus jumped off the stairs, gathering steam with every step he took. "She treated me like the scum of the earth," he bellowed, waving a tight fist under the sheriff's nose.

Chris assessed the man with interest, but he kept his own counsel. Gus seemed more concerned with retribution than in his wife's murder. It hadn't been too much love spilled between the two of them.

"Don't you think we should see about Lorna first, Gus?" the sheriff inquired, not without sarcasm in his voice. "Your wife lies dead on your kitchen floor, and you're looking for satisfaction, I see. That doesn't vouch too much for you," he continued, spearing Gus with his words, and neither Gus nor Chris missed the unspoken threat in the sheriff's words.

"Kenneth Willow," Gus exclaimed, "you can't believe that I've had anything to do with Lorna's death."

Gus's eyes bulged, ready to pop out of their sockets. The dampness of his palms intensified, and when he wiped them off on his shirt, they left a wet trace. He bit his bottom lip uncontrollably.

Kenneth just shrugged indifferently, happy that he had derailed the conversation from Norma Jean. Then, he turned to Chris, "Henderson, do you have anything in your car? Like yellow paint, forensic kit, you know, the works?"

Chris stared at him, startled. He shook his head to clear it and inquired, "Shouldn't we call OSBI[1], Sheriff? It's a murder, after all."

He was pretty sure that no one in the sheriff's office had the necessary training to investigate a murder, and, definitely, not the sheriff. He couldn't find his head if he had to look for it.

"We don't need them," Kenneth replied in a hard voice, dismissing his words off-hand. "Do you have the kit or not?" he barked.

---

[1] Oklahoma State Bureau of Investigation

His blood pressure had already raised a notch during the confrontation with Gus, and his face had slightly colored. Henderson's suggestion just made things worse.

Chris nodded, and after a brief hesitation, he went to the car to bring the kit. He doubted that the sheriff knew what he was doing, and he didn't like to think of the mess to follow. He decided to keep himself as far as possible from any subsequent disaster. Otherwise, his career would have ended before it had had the chance to start.

Kenneth followed him with small and hard eyes. He had never liked that Henderson. The man reasoned too much and had too much common sense. Now that Lorna was gone, Henderson was in a stable position to take the sheriff's place, and his hatred for his young deputy rose.

CHAPTER 5 – AN INVESTIGATION WITH ACCENTS OF VAUDEVILLE

Kenneth started the investigation in force. He marched into the house, disinterested in the footprints that marred the wooden floor of the hall.

I'll clean my boots later. Or better yet, I'll ask that darn Norma Jean to do it. She owes me, and big time.

Kenneth stomped into the kitchen, his boots covering the bloody prints.

Chris followed him, shaking his head. He cringed every time the sheriff stomped over one of the footprints.

Kenneth Willow was like an elephant in a china shop. Anyone who had watched a CSI episode, no matter which one, would have known not to destroy the evidence.

It seemed that the sheriff wasn't a fan of the respective TV series. His actions spoke louder than any of his previous vicious declarations about the shows.

The sheriff got into the kitchen and braced one hand on the table.

God knows what prints were there, Chris thought, and then he cringed inside once more. He shook his head but kept his mouth shut. If the man wanted more rope to hang himself, he wasn't going to stop him. Kenneth Willow was the boss, after all.

Kenneth stared at the body for a few minutes. Open fascination marked his features. The silence stretched, and Chris wondered what the sheriff saw or thought, although he doubted the man's reasoning powers rated very high on any measuring scale. At least, he had never noticed anything of the kind.

A fly buzzed by and disturbed Kenneth's trance. He straightened, and to Chris's bafflement, he nudged Lorna's leg with his pointy boot, and not too gently either.

That was going too far, and Chris couldn't hold his tongue anymore. The sheriff's actions nudged him to inquire, "What are you doing, sheriff?" It was one thing to contaminate the evidence and another to kick the dead.

"Making sure she's not faking," Kenneth answered in earnest, keeping his eyes trained on the body, and Chris's brows shot up to his forehead.

"I doubt Mrs. Carter's faking, sir," he disputed the sheriff's observation, shaking his head again. He became aware of doing that often around his boss. "Not with all that blood and the knife protruding from her abdomen," he pointed to the body.

"Then you don't know Lorna," Kenneth dismissed him with a wave of his hand. *The pup! He thinks he knows everything about life and has no idea what's going on before his eyes*, he thought. "That woman's capable of anything, Henderson. You can't imagine to what lengths the shrew would go to crush someone."

"To crush someone?" Chris repeated in disbelief, and his face showed that he thought the sheriff had lost his senses.

"Yeah, she would if she wanted someone convicted for her murder," Ken assured him with confidence.

The man's sanity is long gone, the deputy thought. He wanted to hold his tongue but couldn't.

"I don't think she'd like to stay dead just to *crush* someone," he noticed with heavy sarcasm in his voice.

The sheriff's ears didn't miss the hint of sarcasm in the deputy's voice, and he turned to him with hard eyes. He pressed his lips in a tight line and stared at him for a few seconds.

"Don't overload your mind, kid," he said glibly after a few moments.

The deputy blushed furiously. He was younger than the sheriff, but he wasn't wet behind his ears. And, anyway, any sane person would have seen that there wasn't any sign of life in Lorna's body. Besides, the sheriff's reasoning was flawed. Faking a death didn't lead to anyone's conviction.

"Let's look around and gather the evidence. We've wasted enough time, and I want to get some sleep tonight. You start with the body," the sheriff ordered to the deputy.

"With the body?" Chris asked with bewilderment and braced his hands on his hips.

"You have dust in your ears, boy?" Kenneth barked. "Yes, with the body," he repeated in a voice that didn't leave room for arguments.

"Shouldn't we call a medical examiner before touching the body?" Chris dared to ask.

He had watched every single CSI series. He wasn't the man to show preference to one over the other. He knew what he was talking about now because he had learned a lot. He hadn't just wasted time in front of the TV. He dreamed of making a career in law enforcement, and being a deputy was only the first step.

The sheriff looked at him as if he lost his mind, "What for?"

"There might be evidence on the body that only a coroner could ascertain," the deputy replied emphatically. Chris knew that his reply would flare the sheriff's rage, but he didn't have time for tact.

There might be evidence on the body that only a coroner could ascertain, the sheriff mimicked his words, and then said with misplaced superiority, "How much smarter is a coroner than us?"

He thought that he had phrased the question quite nicely, to prick the deputy's pride. No man would admit that there was someone else smarter than he was.

"About this..." Chris said, pointing to the body, "much smarter."

That trumped the sheriff's expectations. The man gnashed his teeth and tried to smother his urge to slap the young pup over the head. The compulsion had gotten stronger, but it wouldn't do to strike a subordinate.

"Maybe for you," he replied tartly. "Now, start and gather that damn evidence," he exploded. Losing his temper, he threw a plastic bag to the deputy.

"What do you want me to put in this bag?" Chris asked mulishly, determined not to let the discussion go without aggravating the sheriff only a little more.

Anyway, it wasn't like he had the intention of collecting any evidence. The sheriff could go to hell with Chris's warm wishes. The deputy didn't dare ruin a murder investigation with stupid actions. He knew that his future would go down the drain in the process, as well.

"That knife, for instance," Kenneth said through his teeth, and his strained voice betrayed his impatience and anger.

"I need gloves," the deputy replied stubbornly, only to stir up the older man's anger.

He didn't know what pushed him to do that, but the impulse was stronger than his prudence. Besides, he relished every shadow which crossed the sheriff's face and every sound that proved that the man was gritting his teeth to powder.

"What for?" Ken barked with exasperation. "Your mind has absolutely turned to mush ever since you started watching those silly CSI dramas, you are speaking about all the time. That's a film, boy., and this is real life," Ken said, pointing to Lorna's body lying on the floor. "Put the dang knife in a bag and seal it," he bellowed, losing his temper. Ken's face had already turned scarlet, and his blood pressure went up another notch.

The deputy looked at him sideways and said, "You know what, Sheriff, you want that knife in the bag, you do it. I might be younger than you by about twenty years, but I didn't come with the bees the other day. How stupid do you think I am to leave my prints on that knife?"

"Whaaat?" Kenneth exploded. The man couldn't believe his ears. The pup had refused to obey an order, and that wasn't acceptable by any standards.

Chris turned to leave the kitchen but stopped to throw over his shoulder, "By the way, I do wonder why you insist that I touch that knife, and why you don't want the medical examiner here. Something's fishy if you ask me," he concluded, tapping his nose with his forefinger. Then, he left the kitchen swiftly despite his build.

Kenneth looked after him completely befuddled, his eyes bulging out. "I didn't ask you, you...you... You're fired, do you hear me?" he yelled loud enough to draw Gus to the kitchen.

"What the heck's going on, Ken?" he asked the sheriff.

"That snot-nosed kid," Kenneth mumbled, and his fist connected with the wall. He winced and hissed when the pain registered in his brain.

"What about him? Speak up, man. I can't hear you," Gus prodded impatiently. At the same time, he eyed the wall dubiously, where the sheriff's fist had left a sizeable hole. He had the idea to ask him to pay for fixing that.

"He saw those CSI movies and thinks he's a big shot. He wants me to call a medical examiner and wear gloves...," Kenneth complained loudly, but Gus interrupted him.

"You mean to say that you haven't called a coroner? And you aren't wearing gloves? What the heck, are you thinking, Ken? You want to mess up this investigation, or what? I won't have it, do you hear me?" he bellowed his outrage at the top of his lungs.

"What are you saying?" Kenneth asked with suspicion in his voice.

"Call the darn coroner, man," Gus yelled, out of control now. That Sunday evening was getting worse and worse, and he had already had enough. "Or **I** will have OSBI called," he threatened. "I told that darn woman you weren't good for a sheriff," Gus said, gritting his teeth and shaking his head. "You're good to bully, Kenneth Willow, but you don't have the brains for the job," he pointed out, and one of his thick fingers poked Ken's chest.

Ken's face turned violet now. No one had ever talked to him that way, especially since he became the sheriff of that God-forsaken town. He was the law in that district, and people feared him.

"I think I'll arrest you, Gus" Ken found his voice and pushed Gus's fat finger away. "You are the best suspect in this case," he concluded with conviction, ready to give Gus a taste of his own medicine.

"Oh, you have a suspect list now," Gus said ironically. "Don't overtax your brain too much, Kenneth," he laughed mirthlessly. "Let me call my lawyer, sheriff. I'm sure he'll take care of your sorry hide," he added and picked up the phone on the wall.

CHAPTER 6 – OSBI AT THE SCENE

Within the hour, Orchids Street witnessed more activity than in a year. The OSBI agents came in two cars, and the medical examiner arrived in the county morgue truck. Another car brought the forensic experts Kenneth despised so much.

His hands clenched in tight fists on his hips, Ken stood by the opulent staircase in front of the Carters' house. He didn't move a muscle, but his eyes surveyed everything.

His mind had been in constant turmoil since Henderson refused to help with the collection of the evidence, and Gus insisted that the deputy remained at the scene. Gus didn't seem to trust Kenneth not to spoil the evidence.

Kenneth hadn't seen the deputy since he left the kitchen, though, and he hoped that Chris had gone back to the station.

The sheriff hated Chris Henderson because he hadn't followed his orders and, even worse, had called him a fool. Yet, his hatred for Gus was stronger.

An hour earlier, under Kenneth's baffled eyes, Gus had called his lawyer and explained the situation. He had enjoyed considerably describing Ken's idea of a murder investigation and the muddle he had made. George Hamilton, Gus's lawyer, was a prominent jackal and had powerful connections. He had immediately reached out to the district attorney, who asked OSBI to come and take over Lorna's murder investigation.

And just like that, Kenneth's hour of glory had vanished. He had seen himself becoming the most famous investigator in the state. At the thought of the lost opportunity, his fists tightened a fraction more, and his teeth clenched.

A thirty-some-year-old man left the group of people gathered near the parked cars in the street and came toward Kenneth. The sheriff assessed the man's clothing and smirked. It was the usual cheap suit worn by special agents, regardless of the agency.

A bitter taste of bile reached Ken's mouth. Ken had fantasized about becoming a special agent himself once, but he hadn't made it. He had failed the first test and hadn't dared to try it again. His wife had said to Ken, in not very kind words, that he wasn't made to be one. So, she had advised him to find something to do in the little backwater town, and that was what Ken had done.

"I'm Assistant Special Agent in Charge, Morgan Mackinnon," the man introduced himself politely and stretched his hand out to the sheriff.

Kenneth pretended not to see the man's hand. It was a narrow-minded gesture, but, that night, any reasonable thought had disappeared from his head.

He eyed the man with open displeasure. *Assistant Special Agent in Charge, I'll show you what's so special about you.* Yet, Ken had enough lucidity left not to say it out loud, although he loathed the agent's thick head of dark brown hair and height. The man was everything he wasn't.

"Agent," Ken said, greeting the man with a shallow bow of his head. The special agent was much younger, and he didn't care to dignify him with too much show of respect.

The light from the headlights shone over Ken's bald head. He had forgotten his hat on the Carters' kitchen table, where he had thrown it while planning the investigation of all times.

Mackinnon likened the man's head to a bowling ball, and a subtle smile fluttered on his lips for a few seconds. The sheriff noticed the flitting grin, and his mouth turned into a hard line.

Mackinnon assessed Kenneth Willow with a cold eye. He knew the man had been a sheriff for about ten years, although the agent questioned the wisdom of his re-election, time after time.

The prosecutor had already told Mackinnon what happened in the victim's house before he had called OSBI on the investigation. The agent couldn't decide yet if the sheriff was plain stupid or had tried to cover up a murder.

"I understand you have a crime on your hands, Sheriff," the agent said, without showing any visible sign that he had noticed Ken's rudeness. He burrowed his hands in his pant pockets and stood before the sheriff with a self-assurance that grated the older man.

"On my hands?" Ken spluttered. "What do you mean? You don't believe that old fool, do you?" he asked, and despite his attempt to control himself, his hands shook, and his knees turned weak.

"Believe that old fool?" Mackinnon inquired, raising his right eyebrow.

"Gus," Ken hurried to say, flapping his hands like a big bird of prey. "I know he told that lawyer of his that he thought I'd killed Lorna."

Ken Willow's indignation appeared genuine. However, Mackinnon didn't want to rule anything out yet.

"Oh, I see now," the agent said in a soft tone of voice. "Well, no, I wasn't talking about that. I said that you had a murder in your back yard, meaning here, in your town," he explained, waving his right hand around to encompass the neighboring streets.

Ken wiped his forehead with his meaty hand. The agent had already noticed that the sheriff and Gus shared some features, and unfortunately, the unpleasant ones, like the beer-gut and a sense of superiority, which surpassed common sense.

"Well, maybe, you can tell me what you discovered and how you directed your investigation," the agent suggested, and then glanced to the right where his people came into his peripheral view. Three agents and the medical examiner had joined them.

"And I'd like to see the body," the coroner said in a hard voice, watching Ken unflinchingly. He had already heard about the disturbance of the crime scene, and the contamination of the body. "Who touched the body?" he asked, and a sick feeling squeezed Ken's heart.

The coroner was an older man, but his authority was incontestable. Ken didn't do well with people like him because he knew that he wasn't able to bully them into submission. Consequently, he feared and detested them at the same time.

"I... I don't know," he confessed, and his voice shook. "I... might have touched a leg...," Ken stammered, not sure how to admit that he had touched the body with his boot.

"I'll find out anyway," the man replied with conviction, and Ken's face flushed. "You certainly touched the body," the medical examiner concluded. He could read the sheriff's guilt all over his face.

"I... wanted to make sure that she was dead," Ken admitted, and the others frowned when his words registered.

"I understand that someone stabbed the woman several times," Mackinnon expressed his befuddlement.

"Yes, she was, but..."

"Did you see her breathe?" another agent asked.

"No, but..."

"But what, man? Speak up," the doctor lost his patience. "If someone stabbed her several times, and you didn't see her breathe, what made you verify if she was alive?"

"She might have faked it," the sheriff admitted in a near shout, and everyone's face fell.

The man's explanation was something they hadn't heard too often. Mackinnon, at least, had never heard it before, and considering the expression on the coroner's face, he hadn't, either.

"He's telling the truth," Chris Henderson intervened, and everyone turned to him with similar stunned expressions.

The sheriff speared Chris with a black look. He thought that Henderson had left even though Gus had insisted he stay. Ken didn't want his deputy around.

"Are you for real?" a young female agent asked, although her wide eyes peered not only at the deputy's face. His broad chest received equal attention, as well.

"That's what he told me at the time. So, I don't think that he's lying about his intentions, at least," Chris replied with a shrug.

I'd thank you not to help, the sheriff thought bitterly but said, "Yes, that's why I touched the body. Just with the tip of my boot," he said, and then, he realized that he made a mistake.

The horror on the agents' faces was unmistakable. Mackinnon shook his head. The unreality of the night was overwhelming. They had had gruesome cases to solve before, but, at least, they hadn't had to put up with people like the sheriff.

"You mean to say that you nudged the body with your boot because you thought that the woman was faking," he said slowly, merely to clarify the sheriff's confession, and noticed that all the others were shaking their heads, as well. He wasn't the only one who found that confession ludicrous.

"Yes," Ken repeated. "I know what you think," he broke out, his face scarlet once more. Ken felt ridiculous, but he knew he was right. "You don't know Lorna Carter, but I do," the sheriff continued to say.

"I suppose that Lorna Carter's the victim," Mackinnon interrupted him.

"Exactly," Ken spit out, furious with his interruption. "She'd be able to fake her death only to have someone convicted of the crime. She was a tough broad."

"But there's an error in your reasoning, sheriff," Chris Henderson interjected, and the sheriff wanted to curl his fingers around the man's neck and throttle him. That Henderson had turned out to be a pain in the ass. Ken cursed the day when he had hired him.

"To get someone convicted, Lorna had to be dead, go through the post-mortem, and then get buried. Even Lorna wouldn't have gone so far," the deputy pointed out, counting on his fingers.

Chris had the satisfaction to see the sheriff's eyes bulge again, which was partly his purpose. Henderson was a nice guy but not a doormat. He could give as much as he got.

Ken Willow swallowed hard. He hadn't gone so far in his analysis, and now, he felt like Joe, the town fool, who was the laughingstock of most of the children in their town. His shoulders stooped as if he were defeated. A vein throbbed in his temple, ready to burst, his vision blurred, and his hands shook.

The sheriff found the strength to skirt round the group of agents, and with stiff legs, he went to his car. He threw over the shoulder, "Henderson will help. He knows what's what. I'll be in the office tomorrow."

The group of investigators looked at his retreating form until he got into the car, and then they headed to the house, Henderson showing them the way.

CHAPTER 7 – NO USE TO CRY OVER SPILLED MILK

"There are bloody footprints in the hall, all the way to the kitchen," Chris explained to the investigators while leading them up the stairs. "I don't know how useful they are now, though," he said, shaking his head with regret. "The sheriff walked all over them, I'm afraid. Nothing to do about that now."

"So, you're the deputy, I understand," Mackinnon said and assessed the young man with sharp eyes.

He didn't miss Chris Henderson's eagerness. He also appreciated the young man's unexpected wisdom in dealing with the crime scene. Considering the sheriff's performance, he had to commend the deputy.

Mackinnon imagined that they hadn't witnessed such a crime for generations in that small town. That wasn't an excuse for the sheriff's behavior, though, but explained the things somewhat.

"Oh, yes," Chris blushed under his scrutiny. He was in the company of his idols, and they were talking to him. His heart swelled whenever he thought of that.

Chris hadn't expected that they would pay any attention to him. After all, he didn't have the experience and training to fall back on, and he was a mere deputy in a small forgotten town. And yet, surprisingly, they treated him as an equal and asked him all sorts of questions. His heart burst with pride. It was no wonder that he had forgotten his name.

"I failed to introduce myself," he suddenly said and pushed his stretched hand to Mackinnon. "I'm Chris Henderson."

Mackinnon shook his hand and smiled thinly at the eager deputy. *Not another one, Lord,* he thought.

He recognized the so-called fans from far away, and, usually, he avoided them. This time, he had nowhere to run. He was stuck there with his investigation and the green deputy in tow.

"So, you've been at the scene already," he observed. He needed to direct their discussion back on track.

"Yes, I was the first to get here. I came after Mr. Carter called the office to announce the murder," he answered readily. "Norma Jean took the call. She's our dispatcher," he added breathlessly.

He stopped when he became aware of his agitation and excitement. He didn't have to bring Norma Jean into the conversation. It wasn't relevant to the case.

"Then you can tell us what changes occurred in the scene between the moment you came and now," the other female investigator noted.

Chris glanced at her politely, but then he did a double-take. His astonished eyes rested on the swell of her breasts, and he licked his lower lip unconsciously.

Mackinnon cleared his throat, and Chris turned his head as if he were caught doing the nasty. A faint blush covered his cheekbones and the tips of his ears. The agent found that very telling.

"I suppose so," Chris found his voice, after clearing his throat a few times. "If the sheriff didn't do anything else after I left the kitchen, I mean," he specified. It wouldn't do to mislead them.

"We'll find out soon enough," Mackinnon said with kindliness, to make Chris feel at ease, and then, he tapped him friendly on the shoulder. He had seen where the deputy's eyes had stopped a few moments before, but he had to admit that the young man had a valid reason, even though it wasn't a very gracious one.

Agent Kate Williams was remarkably curvacious in some areas. Usually, men needed some time to become used to seeing Kate and react normally.

Mackinnon had even balked at having her on his team when she transferred there. He had thought that she would be a constant distraction, even for him, at least in the beginning. Thank God, he had passed over that distraction fast enough.

Before getting into the house, the agents covered their footwear, and Mackinnon signaled Henderson to follow suit.

Kate Williams started snapping pictures with the digital camera she had brought with her from the car. She carefully photographed every single detail of the house.

The other female investigator, whose name Chris Henderson hadn't heard yet, turned her attention to the blood smeared on the wooden floors. She collected samples and at the same time, placed cards with numbers next to each footprint so that Kate could record it with her digital camera.

"I hear Lorna Carter kept a clean house," Henderson remarked idly. He didn't address anyone in particular. "I think that would help with prints and such. When she left the church at noon today, I heard her talking to her best friend. Lorna told her that she'd cleaned the house to an inch of her life the other day, whatever that might mean..." Chris said thoughtfully, tilting his head in confusion. Then he shrugged as if he gave up considering the matter. "Anyway, I think it means that she cleaned house just yesterday afternoon," he continued.

Even though he knew that he was rambling, Chris couldn't stop. He wondered if anyone listened to him, though, and his awkwardness echoed in his voice.

With a hint of a smile in the corner of his mouth, Mackinnon tapped him friendly on the shoulder again and said, "It will help, you're right. Let's see the body now," he invited Chris to show them the way.

Chris entered the kitchen before the agents and looked around attentively. "I think everything's the same. I mean, when I left, the kitchen looked pretty much like that. I didn't touch anything in here, but the sheriff leaned on the kitchen table, there," he pointed to where Ken's hand had touched the side of the table. "I suppose Gus touched the phone on the wall there when he called his lawyer. Of course, I don't know if the sheriff stepped in the blood near the body, but it is possible," he admitted. "Oh, that wall there didn't look like that. It looks like someone drove a fist into it. Probably, the sheriff," Chris guessed. "I don't see Gus doing something like that. He's a calm man, normally."

The frown on Henderson's face deepened as he was trying to remember other things. Then he noticed that the agents had engaged in something else and doubted that they heard his words even if he talked.

The coroner, with a frown between his eyebrows, stared at the corpse, his legs apart, and his hands on his hips, and then bit his lower lip and seemed lost in thought.

"Something's wrong, Doc?" Mackinnon came to the doctor and asked when he noticed his preoccupation.

The coroner shook his head. "I utterly can't understand how that man could have believed that the woman was faking her death. Any rational being would have seen that she was dead. Look at her! Look how many wounds are there," he pointed to the body, which, indeed, had been stabbed several times. "No one would survive such injuries, Morgan. The blade must have punctured the heart right there," he pointed to a very angry wound. "And how come he couldn't see the knife protruding from her abdomen is beyond my comprehension," he shook his head.

"I get your point," the agent replied, nodding. "Yet, there's no account for what people might think, is there, Mick?"

Mick, the coroner, nodded. They had had their share of lunatics over the years. Yet, he hadn't expected something like that from a sheriff.

He hunched next to the body and opened his kit. After he pulled up a pair of latex gloves, he started his work in silence.

Morgan Mackinnon stared at the body for a few moments. He wanted to memorize everything for future analysis, even though Kate had already taken photos before the coroner touched the body.

Then, the agent looked around carefully. His trained eyes searched for clues the killer might have, unintentionally, left behind. Experience had taught him a few things, especially that a murderer always left something behind at a crime scene. The problem was only to recognize that something.

David Donaldson, one of the agents under his supervision, approached him.

"There's no sign of forced entry at the front or back door, boss," he reported to Mackinnon. "Whoever did this was invited inside. No one broke in. There's no sign of struggle anywhere, and I checked all the rooms here downstairs. The living room and dining room look undisturbed. It's like no one is living here, boss," he said, shaking his head.

Something had struck David as odd, Mackinnon could tell. The man was puzzled, and usually, he found an explanation in everything. Not always the correct one, but at least he tried.

"Not even a piece of paper or magazine or anything in sight. Someone has tucked everything away. The rooms are just ready for guests," he explained, and his eyes shone with astonishment.

Morgan had to keep his amusement in check. He finally understood and tried to imagine how David's apartment looked.

David was a confirmed bachelor. Some said a convinced one. That didn't mean that he was immune to the fairer sex. David liked the women's company, and maybe too much. His problem was he couldn't do with a steady relationship. David loved the variety in his romantic life. A lot of diversity was closer to the truth.

The man was about the same age as the deputy, Chris Henderson, yet their similarities ended there. Chris Henderson seemed to be more grounded in some ways than David. He was more mature, despite his lack of a broader horizon, as a result of living his entire life in the confines of that small town.

Mackinnon couldn't see Henderson wooing a girl now and another one after fifteen minutes, either. Even physically, they were opposites. Chris was tall and broad-shouldered while David was lanky. Chris's thick, unruly black hair shadowed the agent's quite short, thin blond hair.

Morgan had already noticed the envy in David's eyes, whenever Kate or Nancy stole looks at Chris, and they did that almost every few minutes. If he hadn't known how hardworking the two female agents were, Morgan would have snapped at them. For him, they could look at the deputy to their hearts' leisure, as long as they worked. He didn't mind.

On the other hand, David had never impressed the two agents, although he had made serious efforts. Jealousy and envy made David scowl at the poor deputy the whole time.

Morgan's smile broadened when he noticed Henderson's confusion. The deputy didn't understand why David kept giving him the evil eye. He didn't seem aware of his attraction and good looks.

"All right, David, check the upstairs as well, although I doubt there's anything relevant there," he told the agent. He didn't like the staring contest between the two young men and decided to end it.

David nodded briefly and left the room, not without throwing another mean look in Henderson's direction. The deputy shrugged indifferently, as he didn't understand what the agent had against him, and turned his eyes on Mackinnon. He was eager to learn everything he could from the Special Agent in Charge.

Mackinnon mused and then addressed the coroner, "So, Mick, what can you tell me?"

"Just the obvious, Morgan. Someone stabbed her five times. These three wounds here bled some but very little. The knife had already struck the heart here," Mick, the coroner, pointed to a nasty cut. "However, I might still find a trace of bleeding inside the body," he mentioned.

Mick looked at the body a few more seconds and then shrugged.

"I suppose I could say that it was a crime of passion, either because of blind fury or because of jealousy, although I doubt the latter," he said.

He glanced at the victim's face and frowned, "The woman doesn't seem the type to have aroused great passions in a man. At least, not enough to make him kill her in a feat of jealousy. But what do I know? The world is full of loony people, as you've already remarked earlier," the coroner said and shrugged.

He gathered his things and closed his kit carefully. Then, he stood up and added, "They can take her to the morgue. I'll do the autopsy at ten tomorrow morning. I have another one first thing in the morning. I suppose you can wait until then," he inquired.

Morgan inclined his head in agreement and signaled his other agent, Bob Letzky, who was waiting aside, to have the body removed. Bob went outside to call the morgue assistants to pick up the corpse and returned immediately with them in tow. They bagged the body and took it out to the truck.

Morgan waited for Mick Johnson to leave as well and then turned to Bob, "You and Nancy dust the place and get all available prints. Kate is in charge of the chain of evidence. She's already put the knife on record."

Bob nodded and left to bring Nancy into the kitchen. Mackinnon didn't expect a real answer from him. Bob was a rather quiet man. Mackinnon wasn't sure that he had ever heard more than a dozen sentences coming out of his mouth, and Bob had been working on his team for over six months already.

Anyway, Bob brought some balance to the team. David would talk their ears off all day long. Bob offered some respite.

"Kate," Mackinnon addressed the curvy brunette, "when we finish here, we'll look for some rooms at the motel I saw down the interstate, outside of town."

"I can call them and ask to have the rooms ready for you," Chris intervened. "They close at midnight," he said and glanced at his watch. "They're about to close. I'll call and tell them to open rooms for you and leave the keys inside, all right?" he looked at Mackinnon full of hope.

"Do that," the special agent approved. "Have five rooms readied for us. Tell them we'll be here at least two or three days, although it might be about a week," he admitted.

Chris, happy to help, took his cell phone out of his pant pocket and went out of the kitchen. On his way, he looked up the motel's phone number. He knew the owners, the Potters, an older couple, and was sure he would convince them to prepare five rooms for the agents.

Chris returned to Mackinnon after a quarter of an hour. It hadn't been so simple to make old Frank Potter listen to reason and prepare the rooms.

Luckily, his wife, Allison, heard the discussion and intervened. Otherwise, Chris didn't know what he would do with all the agents.

He could have offered some sleeping space in his house but maybe to two or three of them. His cottage had only a tiny bedroom, kitchen, and a living room.

Chris had planned to build some more rooms but kept putting the project aside. He didn't have any plans to marry yet, so he thought that he would have enough time later.

Chris returned to the kitchen after he finished his discussion with the motel.

"You've arranged everything, I suppose," Mackinnon asked Chris, glancing at him.

"Yes, sir, the rooms are ready. I have the numbers here. You only get inside, and the keys are there on the table in each room," Chris explained to the agent.

"Any problems with that?" Mackinnon asked, judging Chris's face. The heated argument with Frank had brought a lot of color in the deputy's cheeks.

"Some," Chris admitted. "The owner is old and set in his ways..." he shrugged.

"I understand," the agent replied. "It's good you got the rooms, though," he smiled. "I wouldn't have felt like spending the night in the car or going back to headquarters only to come back in a couple of hours."

"I'd have found a solution, sir, no worries. I wouldn't have let you sleep in the car," Chris retorted heatedly.

His eagerness touched Morgan Mackinnon, even though it made him feel some unease at the same time. He squeezed the deputy's shoulder and then asked, "Now, to get back to our case, do you have any idea who might have wanted this woman dead?"

"Huh!" Chris exclaimed, staring at the agent. "Huh!" he repeated. and then, he burst into laughter.

It might have been nervous exhaustion, but the man couldn't stop laughing. He laughed until tears came to his eyes.

The agents were looking at him as if he turned into a troll or something similar.

This town is full of lunatics, Mackinnon thought. *The sheriff kicks the body to see if it's dead. The deputy laughs like a madman when I ask for suspects. God knows what else I encounter tomorrow.* Mackinnon shook his head ruefully.

The agent wondered how to stop Chris's laughter and get to more important and pressing matters. However, Mackinnon needn't worry. Chris stopped by himself.

He wiped his eyes and shook his head to clear it and then said, "I apologize, Special Agent Mackinnon. Truly. But your question..." Chris had to stop again. Another bubble of laughter was trying to make its way out of his mouth. Chris pressed the back of the hand over his lips, and then he bit the interior of his cheek to stop the chuckle.

"I apologize again. I haven't lost my mind, don't worry," Chris specified, glancing from one agent to another. "It's just...your question," he shook his head. "You should have known the victim, sir," Chris said to Mackinnon. "I think it would be easier to find out who didn't hate her. Believe me."

"So, I understand that the victim had multiple enemies," Mackinnon concluded.

"That's an understatement, sir," Chris shook his head. "Over eighty percent of the people in this town hated Lorna Carter. Some hated her a little, and some hated her more. I don't think there was anyone who loved her. Not even Gus," Chris pointed out. "Everybody saw how fed up he was with her. She was... the devil personified if you know what I mean," he said and opened his arms as if he were at a loss for words.

"I see now," Mackinnon said. He sighed and rubbed his forehead. "I think we'd be here for a while," he told his agents. "We'll probably have to book those motel rooms for more than a week," Mackinnon admitted, glancing at Chris. "We'll have to make a list tomorrow... A long one...," he admitted. "For the moment, let's only talk to Gus Carter and retire for the night. It's over midnight already," he continued and glanced briefly at his watch.

CHAPTER 8 – THE TROUBLING DAWN OF THE INVESTIGATION

After a brief and unsatisfactory night spent in a motel room, the agents and Chris Henderson reconvened in the sheriff's office at nine in the morning.

The sheriff wasn't in a better mood that morning. He was even worse than he had been the night before. His eyes were blood-shot, and his cheekbones seemed taut. The grey color of his skin didn't leave any room for speculations about his present health. He hadn't slept well, and the bitter taste on his tongue made him purse his mouth as if he tasted not a lemon but a basket full of lemons.

After a brief discussion, the sheriff grudgingly offered the agents the use of a conference room at the back of the station. He knew that he couldn't refuse them, but he was none too pleased.

The room was a sore sight, indeed. Mackinnon guessed they had used it for parties, and that not very often, considering the filthy state of the floors.

Inside, he noticed some paper plates and cups forgotten in disorder on a side table. A few strings of colored paper still hung from the ceiling. At least, they offered a festive appearance to the neglected room. That area needed all the help it could get.

No one had bothered to clean the room for a long while. Flustered, Chris Henderson swept the floor, while the agents helped, moving the conference table and chairs from the side of the room, where they lined the wall in need of a fresh coating. Then, they dusted them.

The musty smell in the air prompted them to open the windows with haste. Yet, they still spent about half an hour, making small talk right there in front of the windows. The air in the room didn't seem favorable to any investigative work, at least not after only a few hours of sleep.

Mackinnon had spoken to the sheriff and convinced Kenneth Willow to allow Chris Henderson to assist with the investigation. The agent tactfully pointed out that Willow didn't need Henderson's help to run the sheriff's office and also mentioned that he knew that Ken had to take care of the sound functioning of the town. That was why Mackinnon couldn't have asked for his assistance in the investigation.

Kenneth Willow had pretended to accept Mackinnon's convoluted explanation. Yet, he guessed the agent's intentions very well. He hadn't been born yesterday.

Mackinnon wanted to get rid of him, plain and simple. Kenneth had made a fool of himself the other night, and now he had to accept the consequences even though he resented how it felt. Unfortunately, that was Lorna Carter's effect on people.

With a glance at his watch, Mackinnon called his agents to order. It was almost ten by the time they gathered around the conference table.

"All right," Mackinnon said. "The evidence we collected last night is in processing right now," he reminded them of their forensic colleagues.

They had returned with the sealed bags to the headquarters during the night. "I suppose that we won't have an autopsy report before late in the afternoon, so I think that we should start on that list of suspects," he turned to Chris. "I understand that there are a lot of those, but let's try to narrow it down somehow, all right?"

Chris Henderson nodded, although his facial expression showed doubt. He didn't know how it would be possible to do so when almost the entire town had something against Lorna Carter, and most of them had grave reasons.

"We spoke to Gus last evening, and he said that he'd gone to see the mayor because Lorna sent him there," Mackinnon looked up at them after checking his notes. "Of course, we can't ask Lorna, but we can ask the mayor's housekeeper at what time Gus arrived there, and at what time he left. David, you'll visit the mayor's house," he said to the agent.

David knew how to talk to a particular type of woman, and he was the best for that interview.

Henderson observed that David noted something on his pad. *Remember, take notes. Darn, I don't have a book with me. I hadn't thought of that. Should I go and get one?*

Chris didn't know what to do and felt the urge to slap himself. Suddenly, he had an idea.

"Special agent," he began, but Mackinnon interrupted him.

"There's no need for formality, Chris. You can call me Mackinnon, or Morgan if you like," the OSBI agent replied with a broad smile on his lips.

Yeah, sure. I might be a redneck, but I'm not a half-wit. Chris felt like rolling his eyes, but he had passed over the age when such behavior was considered acceptable.

He thought of a compromise. "All right, Mackinnon then," he said. "I thought that I should go and bring some coffee. Norma Jean must have arrived at the office already. Today she's got the morning shift, and usually, she prepares a carafe of coffee in the morning," he explained.

He thought of sneaking outside to steal a pad from Norma Jean's stash if she were amiable, of course. Most of the time, she wasn't.

Mackinnon noticed the light in his people's eyes. After only a few hours of sleep, the coffee they bought on the road to the sheriff's office hadn't been enough to fuel their minds.

"That's not a bad idea," he said, and a general sigh of relief burst into the room. "We'll wait for you."

Henderson left the conference room and steeled himself for the discussion with Norma Jean. The woman was contrary on any given day, and unquestionably, she wouldn't be willing to share the coffee with the agents. She had her moments of pettiness, and those moments were more often than Chris would have liked.

Chris returned with a carafe full of coffee and a few paper cups. They had found some in the conference room earlier, but they were full of dust, and they had thrown them away.

Chris had a notebook stashed under his right arm, and Mackinnon grinned. Now, he understood Chris's wish to go out of the room and his offer for coffee.

Mackinnon imagined that Chris's suggestion went against the sheriff's wishes. Ken hadn't offered them a drop that morning. Mackinnon shook his head.

Then, he saw that Chris was incensed but tried to restrain his fury. He hoped that the sheriff wouldn't mistreat the deputy. It wasn't the young man's fault that the agent had chosen him to participate in the investigation.

"No," Chris's terse response came. "It's only Norma Jean," he mumbled, but Mackinnon heard him.

Gus Carter had already told them about Norma Jean, and Mackinnon wanted to have a word with her, as well. The woman seemed to be out of the ordinary, and he couldn't wait to see her. He knew that he would have the chance to meet another dispatcher who treated the callers with so much originality.

Chris gave everyone a paper cup and filled their cups with coffee. Then, he emptied his pockets. He had come prepared with sugar sachets and mini cups with milk.

Both Kate and Nancy smiled at him as if he saved the world single-handedly.

As expected, David scowled at the deputy, and the other agent, Bob, faithful to his usual behavior, didn't show any sign that he cared about anything.

After turning his pockets upside down, Chris took the coffee carafe and excused himself, "I have to bring this back to Norma Jean." *Or the shrew will have my hide.*

When he returned, everyone was stirring their coffee and making small talk. Noticing him, Mackinnon called everyone to order.

"So, let's see, Chris. Who should be on the list? And don't think of a specific order. That will take too long," he warned the deputy.

Chris fluttered his hand and said, "It would be impossible, anyway. I wouldn't know who'd rank higher on the hatred scale. I may have an idea about some people, but not about everyone," he explained.

"So?" Mackinnon cut him short, afraid that the man would keep blabbering, wasting their time.

"Well, let's start with the one that's evident, Gus Carter," Chris proposed.

"Carter? He doesn't seem aggressive," David said only to bring Chris down a notch. His dislike for the deputy was palpable.

"If only aggressive people committed murders, the investigations would be easier, wouldn't they?" Chris inquired, and Mackinnon had to congratulate him, silently, for his comeback.

"What about Carter?" Nancy asked, sipping from her cup.

"When they were young, the Carters, Gus's parents, were the richest in the county. You know, high cotton," Chris gesticulated. "Their wealth has declined somewhat now. Gus made some bad investments, and Lorna liked to spend, and big-time," Chris explained, always with broad gestures.

Then he noticed the annoyance in Mackinnon's eyes and realized that he had strayed from the subject. He clenched his fists to ease off the stress so that he wouldn't babble like an inexperienced boy.

"Anyway," Chris hurried to get back on track, "my granny said that Lorna wanted that wealth and status for herself. She couldn't have had it unless she had married Gus. At the time, there wasn't anybody in the county of the same... caliber. So, during the summer vacation she turned seventeen, Lorna persuaded her parents to leave her alone at home over the weekend," he said.

Then Chris made a short pause and glanced at the people gathered around the table to see if they were listening to him. Satisfied, he resumed his story.

"I understand that Lorna's parents always did and gave her everything she wanted. So, they left her at home alone, and she organized a private party at the house. She invited only a few couples ... You know, some close friends of hers, and of course, Gus. He was the reason for the party, after all," Chris said with eloquence.

Once more, he stopped and looked from one agent to another.

"Lorna's friends made Gus drink... a lot," Chris pointed out. "It was like a dare or something. Granny wasn't quite sure," he waved his hand as if it weren't significant. "Gus whined about that for months afterward... Anyway, the next morning, Gus woke up in Lorna's bed. She was next to him, and the bedsheet splattered with blood... Lorna told Gus that he had assaulted her, and of course, she wept a lot... However, people said that Lorna had been with a couple of other guys before... Anyway, within a month, Lorna and Gus got married... He was scared, you see... People say that Lorna's parents said a few things about a statutory rape... And Lorna did make Gus's life a living hell. I don't think that she wanted to punish him or anything, but that's how she was," Chris concluded and shrugged.

"That means that we do have to check that alibi, David," Mackinnon turned to his agent. "And, carefully. It might have taken Gus a few decades to pay Lorna back, but we can't dismiss the hatred he must have felt for her," Mackinnon observed, and David made some quick notes in his book. "So, this is for the husband. Now, any other close people who might have a reason to kill Lorna Carter?" he asked the deputy. "Other family members, for instance."

"Kinfolk? Right now, there's only one family member left, besides Gus, their son, Edward. He's not eighteen yet. There wasn't too much love between Lorna and Edward. Lorna always tried to dictate his decisions, and Edward inherited her mulishness and tartness. No wonder that they didn't get along. The worst happened when Edward fell in love with Emily Logan."

"Why?" Kate asked.

"Lorna said Emily was white trash. She came from the other side of town," Chris explained. "Sweet girl, quite beautiful, I'd say," the deputy admitted, but there wasn't any interest in his voice. "Now, though..." he started and stopped, looking in the distance, a sad expression in his eyes.

"Now what?" David intervened brutally, and now Chris had the certitude the man didn't like him at all. *As if I cared.*

"Someone raped Emily about eight months ago," Chris began his story. "She was attacked when she came back from work one night... She worked part-time, you know... The attacker dragged Emily behind one of the stores... We found her there only in the early hours of the morning. Frantic, her mother had called here... Fortunately, Norma Jean didn't work the night shift then," Chris slipped.

"Anyway," he rushed to cover what he had said, "when we found her, Emily's gotten a broken jaw and a few concussions... We asked the doctor for a rape kit, but the kit got lost," he said.

Then Chris tilted his head to the left and pursed his lips. After a few seconds, he added, "I think that Lorna had got something to do with that, as well, but I don't have any proof," Chris admitted, shaking his head hopelessly. "Anyway, the hospital refused to give Emily the pill... You know, the emergency pill to prevent pregnancy..." Chris said, looking from one to another.

The agents nodded to make him continue.

"Well, when the hospital discharged her, it was too late for her to go somewhere else and get the pill... She's pregnant, in eight months... Although, I've just heard Norma Jean saying something about Emily and a baby. I heard that Emily delivered last night, but I don't know about it firsthand."

"I see," Mackinnon said. "What did Edward say about Emily being raped?"

"Lorna sent Edward on a church mission right before Emily's attack... She wanted to make him forget about the girl. Lorna said that Emily was nothing but white trash. She said that several times and kept saying to everyone that she had higher hopes for her only son... I told you, Edward will be eighteen soon... Lorna considered that he had a big future before him, and I quote, *that little slut wasn't in his future.*"

For a few moments, no one said anything. Kate sipped her coffee, and Bob thought it was a good idea, so he picked up his own.

Mackinnon stared at Chris, ruminating what he had said. David stared at Chris as well, but with other thoughts in mind.

"What happened when Edward came back from that church mission?" Nancy asked.

The silence had become unpleasant, and she needed some noise around, and the sound of her voice fitted the bill.

Chris glanced at her and answered, "Well, I think you should know, first, what happened before he came."

"Why?" David inquired, his eyes flashing at the man he considered his competitor.

Mackinnon speared him with a bleak look. He was getting tired of David's antics.

"Immediately after Emily's rape, Lorna, with the help of her cronies, started vicious rumors about the girl. She said that Emily hadn't been truly raped. Lorna spread gossip about the girl, saying that she'd been selling her favors for a pittance to a lot of men, and what had happened was only a deal gone bad... In a matter of a few days, Emily's got her reputation in ruins. There were a few who tried to counter Lorna's allegations, but they were few and in between," Chris revealed and tapped his fingers on the tabletop. "I, for one, didn't believe a word. I'd have heard about that before if it had been true. I think that many people didn't believe it, but..." Chris trailed his words without finishing his sentence.

"But what, man? Speak up," Kate urged him. She didn't like the suspense. The agent preferred to know what was what.

Chris blushed at her admonishment. He was a man of a few words, and that morning, he had already used his allotment of words for an entire month.

"Few dared to express their opinions," he explained.

"Why?" Mackinnon inquired quietly.

"Everyone here is afraid of Lorna Carter. She's been known to destroy people, careers, marriages... Lorna was like a force of nature," Chris concluded when he remembered the woman's demise.

"I understand that she destroyed Emily's reputation," Mackinnon said. "I suppose Emily would be furious enough to look for some restitution."

Chris shook his head, "I don't think so. She's a child, and..."

"Huh, I saw children who'd done unthinkable things," David remarked gleefully, happy he could pick on Chris again. That prompted the agent in charge to scowl at him again.

"I didn't say that children can't do things," Chris retorted sternly. "I said that she couldn't. She's... I don't know how to describe her, but she's not capable of that."

"Anyone is capable of a crime given the right incentive," David contradicted Chris. "You seem smitten with the girl," he continued, and the irony in his voice wasn't lost on the deputy.

"Are you for real?" Chris asked, nonplussed, and the light in his eyes showed that he couldn't believe his ears. *You are an ass.* "She's a seventeen-year-old. I wouldn't look in that direction even if she were Miss Universe."

Stupid darn prick. You're too big for your britches. You think you're so big and powerful, hiding behind your special agent title. Let's see how you'd do if you were on your own, and I'd plant my fist in your mug.

"And anyway, I prefer women with a little spunk. Beauty's not enough. It fades too soon, and...," Chris opened his arms and shrugged.

Mackinnon hid his smile. He liked the deputy's spirit. Chris might have been in awe with the OSBI agents, but he didn't take anything someone would shovel at him. Chris also knew to pay people back.

"Anyway, as I wanted to say before being interrupted, once more," Chris began in lecture mode and glanced sarcastically at David, "Emily is notably pregnant. The eighth month," he said and showed them with his hands how big her belly was. "Although, if what I heard is correct, she delivered last night. I saw Emily in church yesterday. She was as big as a house, and she was wobbling. I don't think that she'd have had the strength to stab Lorna five times. Maybe once, but not five times," Chris concluded mulishly.

"All right," Mackinnon decided to bring an end to that line of discussion. "We'll verify if Emily gave birth last night, to tie the loose ends, at least. Emily's mother may have wanted revenge, though," he observed.

"It is possible, indeed," Chris nodded. "However, if I recall correctly, she works the afternoon shift at the paper mill in the next town. I doubt that she'd have been able to get to Lorna at around nine, nine-thirty... But we can check," the man conceded.

"Perfect. Now back to that Edward," Mackinnon said and picked up his paper cup to drink some coffee. Then he noticed that he didn't have any coffee left. *Dang. I need at least another cup of this poison this morning.*

Chris interpreted the longing in Mackinnon's eyes correctly and rose.

"I'll go and ask Norma Jean to make another pot."

He didn't wait for the agent's approval but left the room.

CHAPTER 9 – THE FIRE OF DOMESTIC AFFAIRS

After the deputy went out of the room, David wanted to say something, but Mackinnon put up his hand and stopped him.

"We'll wait for the deputy. I reckon he knows the people around here and seems smart enough. We need his input to make sense of this muddling business. If you're afraid that you'll forget what you want to say, David, make a note, and raise your concern later."

His stern tone didn't leave room for discussion, and David nodded his agreement, although his eyes betrayed his displeasure. He made a quick note in his book. *That darn deputy!*

Mackinnon didn't care for David's demeanor and turned to look out the window.

He had just had a glimpse of the thick, old trees lining the parking lot of the station when a shouting match burst on the other side of the door and startled all of them.

"You darn woman. I said I'd give you money to buy another box, didn't I? Although I've already paid for this one. Just make the darn coffee," they heard an exasperated Chris shout at the top of his lungs.

"Yeah?" a woman's voice shouted back. "Like I care. I'm not your slave, Henderson," she continued to raise her voice. "Get it through your thick skull."

"Who the heck said you're a slave, woman? I only asked you to fill that darn coffee maker and make some coffee," the deputy bellowed with exasperation, and Mackinnon's brows climbed up his forehead. He didn't think the man had it in him. "I'd do it myself, but..."

"Do I look like a housekeeper?" she retorted. A peculiar hiss accompanied her words.

"Look here, you ornery viper," Chris lost his temper.

The sound of a fist thumping the top of a table reached the agents' ears, and they glanced at one another with wide eyes. The deputy hadn't seemed to have a temper.

"You work in this office, Norma Jean. Right now, you're doing nothing…" the deputy started to bellow again.

"Who says I'm doing nothing?" the woman interrupted him with another indignant shout.

She was sputtering mad, and Mackinnon started to fear for the deputy's physical integrity. That woman was one crazy cat.

"Don't you see I'm reading the newspaper, you, dim-witted bastard? You don't have a lick of sense," she concluded in a screeching voice.

Her words touched David. A satisfied smile flourished on his lips at the thought that a woman had turned down the hunky deputy. He didn't mind the dressing down Chris was getting. He had a mind to buy that Norma Jean some flowers. She deserved them. After all, she had made his day.

"Very well," Chris shouted back at her, "read your damn paper and let me make the coffee."

"It's my coffee maker," she replied mulishly. "Don't touch it."

The agents waited for Chris's reply, but, to their disappointment, none came. Mackinnon imagined that he would have to make do without another cup of coffee when the woman's screech filled the room.

"What are you doing? Put me down, you, dim-witted swine."

That made Mackinnon react. His agents' expressions reflected his, as well. They couldn't believe that the mild-tempered deputy had attacked a woman.

Mackinnon jumped off his chair, and, in three long hurried strides, he was at the door. He almost pulled the door off its hinges when he opened it. The man didn't stop but advanced to the main room of the station. The scene before his eyes froze him in place.

The deputy had his arms full with a mad cat woman, who was hissing and scratching his forearms. Her legs made repeatedly contact with his thighs, and her pointy heels must have left holes in the man's skin. Chris seemed in pain but didn't let her go until he moved her to another desk, where he threw her on a chair. When he noticed that the woman was about to fall off the chair, he steadied her and said, "Now, stay here and don't interfere with me, Norma Jean, or I'll get mean with you. Get it?"

Norma Jean's green eyes shimmered with excitement.

Mackinnon realized that the woman wasn't in any danger, quite the opposite. Right then, Norma Jean stared at Chris, and a particular type of hunger shone in her eyes.

Chris stomped behind Norma Jean's desk, where a crumpled newspaper had fallen off the table, lying now on the floor. He measured coffee in the coffee maker placed on a shelf behind the desk and pressed the button to turn it on.

Only afterward, Chris turned his head toward the woman he had thrown in the chair a few moments before and glowered at her.

He didn't even notice Mackinnon's arrival in the room, and Norma Jean didn't, either.

Mackinnon returned quietly to the conference room, a whimsical smile on his lips.

So, the even-tempered deputy has a boiling point. Who'd have thought? Mackinnon started whistling and took his seat.

All the agents' eyes asked him silent questions, and Mackinnon waved his hand with nonchalance. "No big deal, only some... domestic business, let's say. Chris will be back with some coffee in a jiffy."

Mackinnon registered the relieved sighs coming from the agents. David was the only one who frowned. He had expected a little more drama, and probably, he had exulted over the thought that Chris would have to return to the conference room with his tail between his legs.

Oh, jealousy, jealousy, Mackinnon smiled.

CHAPTER 10 - AN EXTENSIVE LIST OF SUSPECTS

Chris returned to the conference room with a carafe of coffee. Without a word, he put it in the middle of the table and then sat down in his chair, his mouth set in a rigid line. A shadow of fury clouded his eyes.

The agents didn't say anything for a few moments and didn't even move. Then, Nancy leaned forward and helped herself to the coffee. The others followed suit. In the next few moments, they all busied themselves with fixing their drinks.

"Let's finish with the list," Mackinnon proposed. "I understand Edward found out what his mother had done when he came back."

"Yes," the deputy answered briefly. "There were a few discussions I heard about," he shrugged. "I don't know if he was upset enough to murder his mother. It seems a little... too extreme."

"Maybe," Mackinnon murmured. "We'll check him anyway."

Chris nodded, although he still felt fired up and couldn't find his place. He leaned back in his chair and rested his right ankle on his left knee. His fingers tapped a staccato rhythm on his thigh.

"Anybody else?" Mackinnon inquired, glancing at the deputy, who suddenly seemed under the weather.

"John Rand," he said. "He's a thirty-four-year-old man, fired from the bakery shop... I should mention that he didn't receive any reference."

"Why was he let go?" Mackinnon asked when Chris didn't add anything else.

The deputy had been more talkative before his dispute with Norma Jean. Now, he seemed somehow subdued, withdrawn.

"Well, he worked for the baker's until he'd insisted on serving someone else before Lorna Carter. Lorna didn't care that the customer had been in the shop before she got there... I heard her saying that she considered herself more than just another customer. Lorna said that she was a pillar of the community, and she couldn't bear Rand's blatant lack of regard... Lorna bullied Jeremiah, the owner, and he fired Rand, without giving him any recommendation... Jeremiah couldn't do anything else. He'd have gone bankrupt in a couple of months... Anyway, Rand couldn't find another job in town or the next... He still doesn't have a job... He also has an old mother to support," Chris explained, turning his palms up. "Lorna didn't care a fig. She said that he'd reaped what he sowed."

"Definitely on the list, boss," Nancy observed, and Mackinnon approved.

"You will interview Rand, Nancy," he told her, and she noted the name consciously in her notebook. "Any other?" he inquired, glancing at the deputy.

Chris scoffed. Mackinnon looked at him inquiringly, and Chris blushed slightly.

"There are too many others," Chris explained his reaction.

"Like who?" David asked, and not without subtle malice. Mackinnon pierced him with a black look, and he looked down, quiet now.

"For instance... Aileen Edwards, twenty-seven, newly divorced," Chris dutifully answered in a monotone tone of voice. "Lorna told her husband, Samuel, that Aileen cheated on him... Even though Samuel knew what kind of woman Lorna was, she planted the doubts in his head. Hence, divorce."

"Why did she turn against Aileen?" Kate asked.

Chris glanced out the window to gather his thoughts and then said, "Lorna had been against helping the group of people that live in the trailer camp at the edge of town. Lorna said that... she didn't see a reason to help a bunch of grimy, uneducated people," Chris glanced back at Mackinnon and shrugged again.

In Mackinnon's opinion, Chris liked to shrug a lot. The agent encouraged him to continue with a slight nod.

"People heard Lorna saying that it was beyond her comprehension, but Aileen insisted it was the Christian thing to do..."

"So, what did Lorna do?" Kate asked him and changed her position in the chair. Now, her long legs were sideways, and David's eyes zeroed in on them, forgetting about the deputy for a few minutes.

Chris tried to recall what exactly happened. Then, he opened his arms wide and said, "The usual… At first, Lorna spread vicious gossip about Aileen… I remember that the town was in an uproar at the time… Just spreading rumors didn't work, so Lorna chose a different approach. She cornered Aileen's husband and told him that she'd seen Aileen with three of the trailer men… Of course, Lorna didn't forget to mention that they seemed pretty chummy… Now, Samuel had his doubts about what Lorna told him, but he already had the idea planted in his head… Soon enough, he divorced Aileen," Chris said.

Then, the deputy glanced at each of them and shook his head.

"It was an ugly divorce," he recalled with a shudder. "Aileen couldn't find anyone to refute Lorna's words... No one could say one way or another, you see..." Chris explained when he read the agents' expression and noticed that they couldn't believe it. "Anyway," he thought to end his story, "Samuel left Aileen almost nothing... Well, she'd remained in the house, but that was a lease."

"What did Aileen do?" Nancy asked with impatience. Caught in the story, she couldn't wait for Chris to continue.

All the agents seemed to enjoy Chris's way of recounting events and looked forward to hearing the end of the story. As Mackinnon expected, Chris shrugged again, and the agent couldn't stop his smile.

Chris finally continued, "Aileen had to look for a job, of course. She still had a house to live in, but she needed to pay rent," he explained wisely. "Aileen found a job only in the next town. No one here in town dared to hire her," Chris grimaced. "Not after Lorna subtly threatened everyone," he pointed out.

"Aileen goes on the list," Mackinnon decided. "I'll interview her," he added and noted her name on his pad. "You will come with me," he told Chris.

Mackinnon couldn't send David to discuss with Eileen if she was so young. David was a hound, and they needed facts and a strong alibi, not a charmed suspect. Bob was helpful when it came to logic. However, he wasn't so good when he had to interview a woman. Mackinnon knew from experience that women answered better to men, so sending Kate or Nancy to talk with Aileen wouldn't have worked either.

"Anyone else?" he asked again, looking straight at Chris.

Chris nodded. Lines appeared on his forehead, showing that he was trying to choose who to introduce to the agents next.

"Oh," he exclaimed and slapped his front. His gesture startled the agents. "I forgot about Matthew Jackson," he excused himself. "He should be somewhere at the top of the list."

"Why?" Bob finally asked his first question, and the deputy rewarded him with a dumbfounded glance. Chris had been sure that the guy couldn't talk.

"Well, he's got two motives," he replied to Bob, yet he didn't continue afterward.

Does he want us to beg? Mackinnon wondered, looking at Chris. *All right, I'll give him a push.* "So?" the agent nudged the deputy to continue.

"Oh, yes," Chris replied as if he just realized that he had stopped talking. "If I recall correctly, Matthew Jackson is about twenty-two," Chris frowned, shaking his head.

That's another one of Chris's quirks, Mackinnon observed.

"Anyway, he'd worked in Carter's auto dealership for a few years when he was let go at Lorna's request. She'd found out that Jackson was in love with Emily... Actually, Matthew had been in love with Emily for years. Everyone knew it. I don't know how Lorna didn't, but... Anyway, everybody saw how Jackson kept his eyes on Emily all the time – puppy eyes, someone said... I don't recall who," Chris shook his head again.

"Jackson hadn't pursued her because Emily was a minor at the time... Well, she still is... but, as I said, his eyes revealed what he felt," Chris said in a voice resembling an old story-teller, and the agents, with David's exception, smiled.

The guy missed his vocation, Mackinnon thought, and playful lights shone in his assessing eyes.

Chris didn't notice. He was paying the same attention to everyone, and his eyes danced from one agent to the other. Chris felt good having their undivided attention. No one had ever paid so much attention to him in the past. Usually, people left him on the sides, and Chris never took center stage.

"When Lorna expressed her opinion about Emily, saying that she was a little slut, Matthew went ballistic," Chris continued. "But truly mad, you know... Like he had a bee in his bonnet... He wasn't too kind to Lorna that day... If I recall correctly, the nicest thing he told her was to mind her own business, because Emily was a good child... He also used a few choice words, like a nosy busybody, and the worst, a woman on a hormones trip... which we translated somehow, but I can't be sure that we did get the gist of his words."

Chris took a brief break and poured some coffee in his paper cup. After all, he had fought for that coffee and deserved to partake in it, as well. He meticulously added two packs of sugar and two mini-cups with milk under the agents' incisive eyes.

I have to reckon that this guy knows how to play a crowd, Mackinnon thought and watched Chris's precise gestures with admiration. *Yep, the guy's much more than meets the eye.*

Chris fixed his drink precisely as he liked it and then sampled it. Satisfied with the taste, he licked his upper lip, a move that Kate observed with a lot of interest.

Then, Chris leaned back in his chair and continued his story, "Now, that was something Lorna couldn't accept, you know. She had her husband fire Jackson immediately, with bad references. Very bad," he nodded as if he wanted to give more weight to his words. "He found a job, though," the deputy shrugged. "He doesn't seem to care about losing his job because of her. Yet, it was obvious that he cared about Lorna's gossip about Emily. She was still doing it, even after the discussion with Jackson," Chris specified.

"All right," Mackinnon said. "Nancy and Bob will tackle Jackson," he glanced at the two agents meaningfully, and they nodded. "Between the two of you, you'll be able to ascertain his guilt or innocence, I hope."

"Who else?" he turned back to Chris.

Chris thought for a few moments, his eyes searching something interesting on the decaying ceiling, and then, he slapped his forehead hard.

The women winced when the sound filled the room, and even David grimaced.

Chris looked back at Mackinnon, "Oh, yes, old Dan Hanson. We can't forget him. Hanson's story is much, much older, but I don't think that he forgot what happened."

"How old?" Bob asked, and Mackinnon couldn't hide his surprise.

Bob had talked again. He asked questions, and twice in the same day. The deputy seemed to have a rather salutary influence on him.

"Dan Hanson had only one daughter... The apple of his eye. I don't remember her name, but we can look it up if necessary. She went to school with Lorna. They were in the same year. Lorna bullied her, big time, you know. I understand that Lorna didn't let the Hanson girl be for one day. Yet, the girl made it to the senior year. Anyhow, the girl fell in love with a boy in the class. He hadn't noticed her until the senior year when she started to blossom. You must understand that's what I heard. I wasn't born yet..."

Mackinnon stifled his laughter and nodded his agreement. He encouraged Chris to continue with a wave of his hand.

"Well, supposedly, Lorna couldn't stand to see Dan Hanson's daughter with that guy, and not because she wanted him. No, Lorna didn't care about him as a man. It was just... a principle, let's say. Anyway, Lorna told the guy that the Hanson girl was... quite loose with her body. Lorna hinted that the girl would even go with two or three guys at a time... Very, very ugly stuff... The guy came to the Hansons' and had a big fight with his girlfriend. He insulted her, and by the end of the quarrel, he left her... Now, the girl was in a pretty bad frame of mind that afternoon. She was alone... Anyway, she wrote a note, explaining what Lorna had done to her during her entire life and ending with the last blow... She left the letter on the kitchen table for her parents to find, and then she went into the barn and hanged herself."

The agents stared at Chris with wide eyes. His stories had been exciting and in a way, quite interesting, chiefly because of Chris's unique way of telling them. Yet, this last story utterly stunned them.

Not even Mackinnon could say a thing. He cleared his throat a few times, and then he was able to articulate a few words.

"Yeah, I see, now, why old Hanson would be a good suspect."

"Dang, I can't be sorry, boss, that someone silenced that woman," David confessed.

Mackinnon didn't answer, but he thought the same thing. Their victim seemed to have been evil reincarnated.

"All right, Chris, we will see Dan Hanson as well," Mackinnon decided. "Now, don't get me wrong, Chris. We do enjoy listening to you, but I'm afraid we'll still be here in this room tomorrow if we continue like this. You'd better write here on this notebook the names of the people who'd have serious reasons to hate Lorna Carter. Next to each name, write the reason succinctly."

Chris felt rejected but complied. He took the pen Mackinnon handed him and started writing his list.

In less than fifteen minutes, Chris returned the notebook to Mackinnon, who read the names aloud.

"Linda Wilson – Lorna drove her son out of town (he was gay); William Miller – lost his job and wife; Mary Davis – Lorna ran over her younger son, and he ended up in a wheelchair; no one punished Lorna; Robert Brown – lost part of his land to Lorna, unjustly; Michael Jones – removed from the town council; John Williams – had a shop; Lorna drove him to bankruptcy; James Smith – spent a year in prison for something he didn't do."

Mackinnon looked at Chris, and the man read the agent's astonishment in his eyes.

"Do you truly mean to say that Lorna did all that?"

"Well, yes. Everything I wrote there is real. I didn't write the names of the people I wasn't sure about," Chris reckoned.

"You mean to say that the folks in this town know what happened to these people whose names you wrote on this paper, and no one did anything?"

Chris looked at Mackinnon through his lashes and then hesitantly replied, "Who could have done what when the sheriff was in Lorna's pocket, and the council trembled in their boots?" Chris ended his litany in almost a shout.

"I see," Mackinnon whispered.

Chris assessed him and noticed that the agent could see, indeed.

Mackinnon laid the notebook before him on the table and took a few moments to think. His fingers drummed the top of the table nervously.

"All right, Nancy and Bob, you take Wilson, Miller, and Davis. Kate and David, you take Brown, Jones, and Williams. The deputy and I will interview Aileen, Hanson, Emily, and Margaret Logan, and Smith. David, don't forget about the housekeeper," Mackinnon reminded David with a stern glance. "Nancy, Kate, and Bob, I count on you to interview the people we've already talked about earlier," Mackinnon said and glanced at his watch.

He grimaced when he saw how late it was.

"All right, people. First, let's have lunch. I saw a diner on Main Street, Chris. Is it any good?"

"Oh, yes. The Robertsons offer the best food in the county. Order the special, and you won't regret it," Chris advised.

"Won't you come with us?" Mackinnon invited him and nearly smiled, seeing the blush covering the deputy's cheekbones.

The deputy nodded. He couldn't articulate words.

CHAPTER 11 – A JUICY LUNCH AND AN INOPPORTUNE BODY

The agents and Chris enjoyed their lunch as well as the entertaining conversation. They reminisced about older cases and answered the deputy's eager questions.

Chris hadn't lied when he told them the Robertsons' restaurant offered the best food in the county. They couldn't recall when and where they had eaten such juicy steaks. Mackinnon even mentioned that being on the road most of the time, they learned to treasure such tasty treats.

Even David started to treat Chris politely, and Bob told a joke that made them all laugh uproariously.

Chris was laughing heartily at Bob's joke when a known screechy voice came from behind him. He was the target.

"Do you think I'm your darn secretary, Henderson?"

Chris turned with a scowl on his lips. He knew that voice very well, and he had had enough of the woman's roaring that day.

"I'm on my lunch break, Norma Jean. What the heck do you want now? If I had my heart's desire, I'd knot your tongue, woman. Your shriek can peel the paint off the walls."

Norma Jean growled and showed him her long red-painted fingernails, ready to jump him. David eyed the woman with interest. She presented an appealing package. Mackinnon was amused but not enough to let the deputy fall prey to her murdering instincts.

"Have you come with business?" he asked Norma Jean, and she turned to him like a cat ready to attack.

Norma Jean controlled herself, though. She thought that it wouldn't do to get into a fight with an OSBI special agent.

"Yeah, I come with some business," she replied tartly. "Frank Potter called," she said.

"The owner of the motel," explained Chris and Norma Jean hissed.

"Am I talking here or what?" she lashed at him.

"By all means," he replied with sarcasm.

Norma Jean rolled her eyes and continued, "So Potter called. A client didn't check out, and he went to ask him if he wanted to pay for one more day. Potter found the client dead on the floor. I suppose he's still there."

No one reacted at first, but then Chris replied sweetly, "I wonder what you said to Potter when he called to announce a crime."

The woman had the delicacy to blush, remembering the previous night, but retorted, "Shut your mouth."

Norma Jean turned on her right heel and left with as much dignity as she could. Chris followed her with his eyes, and a smile fluttered on his lips.

"Two murders in a small community in a row, it is too much to be a coincidence," Mackinnon noticed, and Chris nodded in agreement.

"Especially, if you think that we haven't had any for half a century." the deputy reckoned. "Should we go?" Chris asked Mackinnon. He was confused because the agents continued eating, and none of them seemed ready to go.

"We'll call the coroner and the forensic team first," Mackinnon said. "We can't touch the body or the room before they come, anyway. Kate, you make the calls. I think we have enough time to finish our lunch," Mackinnon concluded in a calm voice. "Maybe you should call Potter and tell him not to let anyone approach the room."

CHAPTER 12 – A TURN OF EVENTS

After exactly forty-five minutes, the entire team was in front of room twelve. Frank Potter waited there for them, his face carved in stone and a deep scowl on his lips. The fingers of his right hand drummed on his thigh, the only sign betraying his impatience. He hadn't liked being told to wait and not let anyone in the room.

Mackinnon stopped before the grumpy man and introduced himself. They shook hands, although Frank's reluctance glimmered in his eyes.

"I'm Assistant Special Agent in Charge, Morgan Mackinnon," he introduced himself pleasantly, but his demeanor didn't alter the other man's. His glower didn't soften.

What the heck is with the people around here? Mackinnon wondered. It felt like a strange déjà-vu after meeting the sheriff the previous night. *It's like I have the plague, darn.*

"Frank Potter," the man grumbled. His voice sounded like sandpaper, and his face showed little enthusiasm for making the agent's acquaintance.

A lanky man over sixty, Frank Potter had a head of white hair. Yet, he still could squeeze a hand.

Mackinnon cringed silently inside but didn't show any discomfort. He didn't want to give any satisfaction to the grumpy man who was watching him thoughtfully.

"When will I get possession of my motel room again?" Frank asked the agent in a quarrelsome voice. It was a well-known fact that pleasantries weren't part of his make-up. "Cleaned, of course," he didn't forget to mention. "I hope you don't expect we'd clean up after you," he glared at the investigator.

As if I'd killed the victim, Mackinnon scoffed, not caring for the older man's behavior. Yet, he said aloud, "You'll get possession of the room once we've removed the body and collected the evidence. It might be between one and three days, though. It depends on the complexity of the case. However," he stressed, "*we are not* responsible for cleaning the room. We'll recommend a few cleaning companies which deal with crime scenes, but that's all we can do," he said in an authoritative voice.

He knew it wouldn't do to show any weakness before the likes of Frank Potter. Such men would have taken full advantage.

To Mackinnon's astonishment, the man sneered at him openly as if the agent had committed a sacrilege. Then, Potter turned on his heel and stomped toward his wife, a woman of similar age, waiting for him in front of the motel's office. The woman's weird orange-dyed hair shone in the bright sun and hurt Mackinnon's eyes.

So, the agent had to close them for a few seconds. Then the agent assessed the woman from the top of her head to the tip of her toes, also adorned with orange nail polish.

Allison Potter's face astounded him. She wasn't how he'd pictured her. A warm smile softened her sun-tanned, parchment-like, and pigmented skin, and the laughter lines etched at the corner of her mouth and eyes belied her kinship with Frank Potter.

Potter had left without a word for the agent. Yet, his mouth ran on and on, even though he didn't speak to anyone in particular.

"*We are not responsible for the cleaning.* Did you hear that? Huh! That's the problem with the world nowadays, listen to me. That's the problem. No one takes responsibility for anything. No one. Not anymore. And that's why a working man can't do a thing but pay and pay and pay," he scoffed until he got to the office.

It was evident that Potter wanted the agent to hear his words because the farther he got from the investigators, the louder he spoke.

Mackinnon's gaze followed the man, but the agent didn't take the bait and didn't reply.

Chris joined Mackinnon in front of the motel room and said, "That's Frank for you. I'm sure that there's no other soul in the district as cantankerous as he is," the deputy shrugged.

"Eh, it doesn't matter," the agent replied. "People get upset when investigations interfere with their livelihood. I can understand it," Mackinnon waved his hand.

The sound of the coroner's car drew the agent's gaze to the street, and Mackinnon noticed that the forensic and morgue trucks had parked behind the doctor's car.

"The doc and forensics are here," he observed. "Now we can start the investigation. Maybe we'll be able to get out of Potter's hair sooner," Mackinnon winked at Chris.

The deputy grinned. "Not that he'd thank you for your consideration," Chris replied. "Even if you cleaned the motel room by yourself, Frank wouldn't bother with a stingy *thank you*," Chris warned Mackinnon.

Mackinnon removed Potter from his thoughts, as if he hadn't been relevant, and greeted the coroner and the other agents.

"I hear that you've got another murder here," the doctor addressed Mackinnon and shook his hand.

At least, one man who doesn't think that I have the pest or God knows what. Mackinnon smiled at Mick Johnson and tapped him on the shoulder.

"Hopefully, it will be the last in this case. It's a small town that hasn't seen a crime before for almost half a century. I don't expect another one," Mackinnon shook his head. But then, he thought better. "Although, I didn't expect this one either," the agent pointed his thumb back to the closed door of the motel room.

"Let's see what's in there," Mick proposed and pulled a pair of latex gloves out of his kit.

Mackinnon followed Mick's example and then wanted to open the door. The agent stopped for a second and commented, "I don't even know why I've donned gloves, though. I am sure that at least two people have already touched the doorknob," Mackinnon shook his head with distress.

The investigation looked somewhat problematical. Suspects popped up all over the place, and no one had come forward with any information, although Chris had already spread the word through the town.

Earlier, Mackinnon had asked about the best way to let the town folk know that he needed them to bring any information to him. Chris had told the agent not to bother. He had a solution.

They were just about to get inside the diner for lunch when Chris exclaimed, "And here's my solution." He merely mentioned the agents' need for information to widow Sorenson, who was passing by the restaurant at the time.

"In less than half an hour, the entire town will know that you're expecting information," Chris assured the skeptical special agent.

"Are you sure?" Mackinnon asked with disbelief. He didn't think that passing the information to one person would do the trick.

'Don't underestimate Mrs. Sorenson," Chris chided friendly, waving his forefinger before the agent's nose. "She's like lightning when it comes to spreading news, rumors, and the like," he nodded with conviction.

At the time, Mackinnon had doubted Chris's solution, but he hadn't expressed his reserves. Now, he reconsidered that.

"Widow Sorenson might be like lightning, but we still don't have any information," he murmured, although only for his ears.

Chris, always on his side, as if the two of them were joined at the hip, heard him just fine and judged his murmur correctly.

Chris replied to the agent warily, "That doesn't mean that Mrs. Sorenson hasn't done her job, Mackinnon. Even Lorna used her as a gossip spreader. Telling something to her is more effective than printing it in the town newspaper. The lack of information means that either there were no

147

witnesses, which seems quite plausible, as I doubt that there was somebody in front of the Carters' home at that hour last night," he pointed with his ever-present shrug, "or they don't want to talk to you, which might very well be the case. People are a mite wary of new people in town."

Mackinnon cursed the man's excellent hearing. *A man can't even think in peace in this God-forsaken town*, he cursed.

Yet, he had to reckon that Chris was right in his assumptions. Mackinnon had often encountered such problems in small towns. People were uptight and didn't trust outsiders, so, if they had difficulties, they solved them themselves. They didn't welcome strangers in their midst and didn't relish to wash their dirty laundry in public.

Mick Johnson, who had hunched near the body and had been checking it for a few minutes already, straightened up and said, "I'd say it's the same murderer. It's a different murder weapon, although also a kitchen knife like the one used on Lorna Carter," he specified.

"What makes you say that it is the same murderer?" Chris inquired with vivid curiosity.

"Well, I won't know for sure until I perform the autopsy, of course, but the depth of the wounds and their angle seem the same," the doctor explained. "The person who murdered this man had the same height and strength as the one who murdered Lorna Carter. I'd say that when the killer stabbed Lorna the first time, he – and I use '*he*' as a generic, mind you - he hesitated. The autopsy revealed that the knife didn't penetrate very deep. However, the murderer either gained more confidence with each wound or garnered more anger. That anger was present here as well," Mick Johnson pointed to the body. "Maybe it escalated, just a notch," he assumed.

"Why do you think that?" Chris asked again.

Mackinnon hid his smile. He knew Mick very well and imagined how he would answer to the enthusiastic young man.

Crossed, the coroner glanced at the deputy. He understood and admired the man's desire to learn, but he wished Chris had chosen someone else to teach him.

Mick Johnson had always refused any offer to teach at the university. He didn't have the patience for the job, and quite a few coroner's assistants could vouch for that.

Despite his displeasure, Mick chose to answer the deputy's inquiry, even though a little irately.

"You can see for yourself, man," he snapped. "It's there, under your nose. Lorna was stabbed five times. With this guy, the murderer lost his temper big time. I think I can see over a dozen wounds," he pointed out. "I'll count them during the autopsy," Mick told Mackinnon, but he didn't bother to soften his tone.

Mackinnon didn't take it personally and expressed his gratitude. He put the agents to work while he read the forensic report. It was incomplete, but it still gave him some insight.

"Hey, Miller," he called to the leader of the forensic team. "I see that you found prints on the knife that killed Lorna Carter."

Short and stout, with a GI haircut, Miller turned to Mackinnon.

"There were only three, but I suspect that they belonged to family members. The same sets of prints were all over the house," he shrugged.

"I see," Mackinnon mumbled. He had hoped that he had a way to pinpoint the murderer. However, Mackinnon had never run away from hard work and wouldn't start doing it right then.

David returned from the motel office and approached Mackinnon. "The Potters showed me the register, boss," David said and wiped his forehead. "It hadn't been easy to convince that Potter guy to show me the ledger without a warrant," he said bitterly. "I swear that the man has seen too many movies. Probably, he's got too much time on his hands."

"Could you get to the point?" Mackinnon asked tersely. He had two murders to solve, and a heartfelt wish to leave that town as soon as possible.

David rushed to answer, "Of course. The man who rented the room... It seems that the victim is the same man... Frank Potter recognized him, despite his... buttonholes," he said. Then he apologized to Mackinnon, "Potter's words, boss, not mine."

"Should I repeat myself?" the agent barked to David. "I said to get to the point."

"Oh, yes," David replied. "Well, the man had a driver's license. His name is... I mean was, Donald Anderson. He used to live in New York, or at least, that's what the driver's license shows. I understand that it wasn't the first time he came around. He'd visit the motel about four or five times a year for the last seven or eight years. The Potters didn't know why and didn't ask. Frank Potter said that he didn't care as long as the man paid his bill in full when he checked in."

"Did you get the dates for his last visits? Let's say three or four?" Mackinnon asked, a thought taking shape in his mind.

"No...," David hesitated. "Should I have...?"

"Of course, you should," Mackinnon said. "Those dates could help us determine why he came here. It's not like the town is renowned for tourism or business," he remarked with sarcasm.

"I'm going back, boss," David said with resignation, and a deep sigh accompanied his hesitant steps. He didn't feel like having his ass chewed up by Frank Potter again.

By the time David got back, looking like a well-wrung dishcloth, Mick Johnson had already had the body removed, and he left as well. Mackinnon had talked to the supervisor of the forensic team. The forensic expert was supposed to analyze the scene and seal the room. The entire investigation team, together with the deputy, was ready to go back to the station to discuss a new plan of attack.

"Have you got the dates?" Mackinnon asked when David appeared.

"Yes, for the last two years, sir," David answered. He had thought to ask the records for a lengthier period because he didn't want to go back and talk to Potter if Mackinnon needed more information for the investigation. David knew that he would have died a happy man if he hadn't ever laid his eyes on Frank Potter.

CHAPTER 13 – THERE'S NO SUCH THING AS COINCIDENCE

Sitting around the conference table once more, the agents consulted their notes and drank coffee. This time they had bought their coffee from a gas station on their way back to town.

Mackinnon had thought it would be better to shop for the coffee themselves than to arouse the wrath of that redhead she-cat, Norma Jean. He feared for the deputy's physical safety. That woman was not one of the southern roses men expected to see in such a little town on the western side of Oklahoma.

Mackinnon called everyone to order when Chris came into the conference room. When they returned to the station, the sheriff had called the deputy to talk to him.

The deputy looked tense, and it was difficult not to notice the way he clenched and unclenched his fists.

"Something wrong?" Mackinnon asked. He was determined to light into the sheriff if he had harassed the deputy for working with OSBI.

Chris fluttered his hand, "Not very important."

He didn't want to rehash the ugly scene in the sheriff's office. Kenneth was spitting mad that the agents didn't rely on him in their investigation, and he took his frustration out on Chris.

"Let's see what we need to do next," Chris proposed and pulled a chair to sit down at the table.

Mackinnon wanted to insist but curbed his tongue. If the man didn't want to share his problems with them, it was his right.

"First of all, we need your help to find a pattern in the victim's visits in your town," he said. "David brought us the list with the dates for the last two years. Let's see," he said.

Then he pulled the notebook where David had written the dates.

"Does the date July 26 tell you something? Think if anything happened around that date. I see Donald Anderson had booked a room between July 26 and July 31," Mackinnon read the dates and glanced at Chris afterward.

The deputy closed his eyes, and lines formed on his forehead. He drummed his fingers on the top of the table and then licked his bottom lip, which attracted the women's attention.

"Two things happened around that time," Chris opened his eyes and spoke. "I remember that one of Randall's cows gave birth to a three-legged calf." Seeing Mackinnon's fixed look, he specified, "Randall has a farm in the north part of the town."

"I don't think that's related to Anderson," Mackinnon remarked drily, and the agents hid their smiles, with David's exception.

"No, I suppose not," Chris shrugged. "The second thing that occurred around that time was the fire at the Whites'. It was a Friday evening, I think. The Whites are farmers, as well. Their barn turned to ashes. They couldn't salvage too much, and poor Mrs. White fell and broke her arm in her rush to take as many things out of the barn as she could. She had severe burns on her arms and torso," Chris remembered with a sad shake of his head. "It was awful. They kept her in the hospital for a few weeks, I think," Chris mentioned, and Mackinnon nodded.

"All right, I understand what happened. Now, can you think of any relation between the Whites and Lorna Carter?" Mackinnon asked Chris on a hunch.

"Now that you ask, I remember that Mrs. Whites did have a serious fight with Lorna a few weeks before the fire," Chris nodded, and his eyes widened when he realized that there was a connection between Lorna and the Whites. "Everybody talked about it. Mrs. White wasn't very gentle. She threw a few unpleasant truths in Lorna's face."

Mackinnon waited a few seconds, and when he was sure Chris had finished giving his account, he glanced back at the notebook.

"What about the period between March 10 and March 14?" he asked the deputy.

The deputy's face darkened, and his eyes turned to slits. He clenched his fists hard, and his knuckles whitened.

"That's when Emily Logan was raped," he replied, almost in a whisper. "We found her in that alley the night between March 11 and March 12."

The dates drew an ugly picture. The deputy's skin had turned grey, and his tension was tangible.

"We could test the baby's DNA," Chris proposed. "Emily did have her baby last night," he continued. "If it matches Anderson's, we have the answer, I think."

Everyone stared at Chris. Mackinnon slapped himself mentally for not having thought of that before.

"You are right, Chris. We'll do that tomorrow. Now, what about December 9 and December 14?" he asked.

Chris needed only a few seconds to remember, "That's when the Wilsons' son disappeared."

"I assume you looked for him," Mackinnon asked.

Chris shook his head.

"No?" the agent inquired, and his disbelief filled the room.

"No," Chris answered in a tired voice. "Lewis Wilson was nineteen at the time. The sheriff said that he'd up and gone, so we didn't do any investigation."

"Should I ask if there was any connection to Lorna?" Mackinnon put the notebook down and looked at Chris.

Chris nodded. "Yes, there was. Just a week before, maybe two, I am not so sure, Lewis Wilson said that Lorna was a bitch, and he'd prove to the entire town what she could do."

"And the sheriff didn't notice that he might have had reasons to investigate the boy's disappearance?"

"The sheriff is the sheriff because of Lorna Carter," Chris pointed out. "He wouldn't have seen any reason to investigate her. Not that he would have seen any connection anyway," Chris mentioned.

He didn't like the sheriff, but he couldn't lie. Ken Willow couldn't boast strong thinking skills. Chris was sure that the sheriff hadn't seen any connection between the Wilson boy's disappearance and his words against Lorna.

Mackinnon stared at Chris for a few moments and drummed his fingers on the notebook. Then, he said, "Chris, I need you to bring me all the information you have about Lewis Wilson. I'll have a team to investigate his case. If the kid is fine and just up and gone on a great adventure, then, great, we'll drop the matter. I'm afraid, though, that his disappearance hides a gruesome outcome."

"One moment," Chris nodded and stood up. He went out of the room, Mackinnon's eyes glued to his back.

"You think that the victim was Lorna's hit guy," Kate told Mackinnon.

"It seems that way, but, first, we'll make sure that we don't see things where they're not," Mackinnon answered. "Plus, I wonder where the heck did the woman find a hitman? I doubt that she found him on Craigslist."

The shadow of a smile curved Bob's lips.

"Something funny, Bob?" Mackinnon asked.

Bob hesitated a few seconds but then said, "You have no idea what you can find on Craigslist, boss."

"Really?" Mackinnon turned to him completely. His eyes sparkled with curiosity. "Do tell me more," he nudged the agent.

Bob opened his mouth to say something when Chris's raised voice penetrated through the closed door.

"Because I said so, you batty woman. And do it now," he barked.

The noise of a stack of files falling on the floor reverberated through the station. Yet, now, Mackinnon knew better than to go and offer his assistance to the redhead virago.

Chris came back into the room with a file in his hand. A muscle was twitching in his jaw, and his lips were pressed in a very tight line. His eyes were so cold that even David shuddered.

"Everything fine, deputy?" Kate asked.

He nodded curtly but didn't offer any clarification.

"This is the file opened for Lewis," he handed the papers to Mackinnon. "It doesn't contain much… Just his parents' account and a photo. I was here when they came and opened the file. In the morning, the sheriff said that it was a waste of time," Chris recalled with sadness.

"Kate, give the information to Albert back at the office and ask him to start investigating this missing kid," Mackinnon pushed the papers to Kate.

The agent gave Albert the information over the phone, while Mackinnon stared at the trees through the window.

When she finished, Mackinnon turned to Chris, "We need to be faster than we've been. Here are the dates," he gave him the notebook. "Tell us briefly if you recall an event associated with the dates, and if there was bad blood between Lorna Carter and the people involved. Bob, you take notes."

Chris looked over the notes in the notebook for a few moments, and then he started to talk.

"This one here, October 3 to October 7, 2015. A car ran over the Campbells' daughter. We've never found the culprit. There's a connection to Lorna, of course. Mrs. Campbell won a competition. Best jam, I think," Chris said.

He glanced back at the notebook. He read the next date and chewed his lips. Then he remembered, "Now, this date, here, May 1 to May 8, 2015. If I remember correctly, we found the Butts' bull in a ravine. No one understood who stole and killed it. I think that the Butts' son got accepted to Yale with a scholarship, and Lorna was livid when she heard," Chris shook his head.

His eyes fell on the book again, and the agents stared at him.

"January 24 – January 29, 2015," Chris said. "I think that was the period when Jeremiah Hicks went to the hospital with multiple fractures. He said that someone jumped him when he got out of the honky-tonk. He'd had a few things to say about Lorna after she destroyed Aileen's marriage," Chris pointed out.

The deputy looked into the book again, brushing his thumb over his chin.

"Yes, here, September 1 – September 4, 2014. That's when we found Thomas Nelson in a ditch with a cranial fracture. He couldn't remember who or what hit him. Thomas lost about a week of his life, and not even now does he know what he did during that week," Chris shrugged. "He doesn't seem too upset because of that, though," the deputy observed. "Probably, because Thomas had been on a rampage against Lorna during the day. Of course, he'd been on a drinking binge at night. That started a month before the attack," Chris said.

"Why?" Mackinnon asked.

Chris shrugged, "Lorna ran his wife out of town. The poor woman was ashamed to show her face around. Thomas's wife was a teacher, and Lorna said that she abused her students sexually. It was ludicrous, you know, but some people believed Lorna, and treated Mrs. Nelson like scum," Chris explained. "Lots of people around here are... you know the saying, *The engine's runnin' but nobody's driving,*" Chris said.

The agents shared a grin for a few moments. They knew the saying.

Then, Mackinnon concluded, "I don't think that we have to go further with this exercise. It's futile. The man killed at the motel was Lorna's hitman. We'll make an extensive list if necessary, but, for the moment, let's conduct a few interviews."

Mackinnon glanced at his watch furtively. "We still have a few hours left to bother the people we have on the list. Kate, besides the people I've already assigned to you, Bob and you will also interview the Whites and the Butts. Chris will give you directions for each of them," he said, looking at Chris, who nodded. "Nancy and David, you will also interview the Campbells and the Hicks. Chris will give you directions, as well. Chris and I will interview Nelson, and of course, the Logans. I already have them on my list. If any of you stumble on something important for the case, call me. If it's only routine and nothing serious comes up, we'll compare notes tomorrow morning," Mackinnon decreed.

Then, he signaled Chris to give the people's addresses to the agents so that they could start the painstaking part of their investigation, the interviews.

CHAPTER 14 - IF EVERYTHING IS COMING YOUR WAY, YOU'RE IN THE WRONG LANE!

"At least we've been lucky to find everyone at home," Mackinnon said to Chris softly. The deputy was out of sorts, and the agent felt like an older brother toward the young man.

Chris didn't think that they had been too lucky. Yes, they had found everyone at home, but they didn't get any information that could help them.

"Don't be so pessimistic," the agent continued. "In this job, there's a lot of waste of time, Chris, and you have to get used to it. You won't get your man immediately," Mackinnon said.

He looked at the deputy sideways and noticed that Chris wasn't convinced.

"I advise you to reconsider if you find your suspect in a second, and you haven't witnessed the crime yourself. If you saw the person committing the crime, then, yes, by all means, that particular suspect is unquestionably the offender. Otherwise, take it easy. You won't have answers in a jiffy, but you will get your man. As long as you're patient and follow the leads, you'll make a good investigator."

Chris kept stubbornly silent. He had hoped to ferret the murderer during one of the interviews, but everyone had an alibi.

"I don't know," Chris finally said. "I'd have thought that old Hanson might have been the man, but he didn't have a reason to out Anderson," he observed.

To out? Where does he come up with these   expressions? Mackinnon wondered.

"Hanson might have thought to impart his brand of justice," Mackinnon replied. "He surely cares about that girl, Emily. If he'd been aware that Anderson raped her, he would have unquestionably done something," he remarked.

"Probably," Chris mumbled. "But then, he was with Emily when Lorna was killed."

168

"There's Nelson left," Mackinnon consoled him. "Let's see what he has to say."

Chris gave him directions to Nelson's house minutely and then kept silent.

Mackinnon turned on the radio to a country station, and Garth Brooks's voice filled the car, singing about friends in low places.

Mackinnon drummed his fingers on the steering wheel to the rhythm of the music, and even Chris tapped his right foot on the car floor unconsciously.

They found Nelson on the veranda with a few long neck empty beer bottles scattered around. He had just thrown another bottle on the floor and bent to pick another one up from his six-pack when they arrived.

He glanced at them and then raised his bottle in greeting. Mackinnon was afraid that the man was too drunk to answer any questions and shook his head.

Chris leaned and said quietly, "Don't worry, he's still able to speak. He's got a lot of training. It would take twice as many bottles to turn him into an idiot," he pointed to the bottles scattered all over the veranda.

The agent wasn't so sure about that, but they had driven to Nelson's house out of town, and he wasn't about to go back to the motel without talking with the man.

"What's up, deputy?" Nelson asked between two mouthfuls. "Has the law changed, and a man can't drink in his own home anymore?"

"Don't worry, Thomas. No law changes this week," Chris grinned at him. "But we do have a few questions for you," he said.

"Huh, I thought so. I wondered why you hadn't come earlier," Nelson said and swung his bottle to his mouth again.

"Why?" Mackinnon asked.

Thomas lowered the bottle and looked at the agent with hazy eyes for a few seconds. Then he waved his hand with disgust.

"What's the problem, Thomas?" Chris asked.

Thomas drank some more beer and then pointed to the agent, "He thinks I'm two bricks shy of a full load."

"Only because I asked why?" Mackinnon inquired.

"You know that there was bad blood between Lorna and me, and the witch deserved what she got," Thomas nodded with conviction and swung the beer to his mouth again.

Then he wiped his mouth with the back of his hand and stared straight in the agent's eyes.

"I've thought about it," Thomas said and ruffled his curly brown hair with the fingers.

"About what, Thomas?" Chris asked, and he felt cold fingers trailing down his spine.

"About closing that woman's mouth for good, of course," the man admitted, and his cold eyes chilled both the deputy and the agent. "And quite often, I reckon," Thomas said unflinchingly.

"I see," Mackinnon murmured only to see if he still could articulate sounds. He had seen tough men before, but that one was cold and unfeeling. If he had been asked, Mackinnon would have chosen Thomas as the leader of the suspects' pack.

"As if I cared," Thomas replied, waving his hand. "Anyway, every evening for the last few months, I'd watch the Carters' house... I get there around eight-thirty and leave around midnight," he confessed.

"Why?" Chris asked and wiped off his hands on his pants.

The evening was unusually hot, and he was sweating like a pig. It was true that Thomas's confessions didn't help, either.

"Because it seemed too convenient," he barked. "And the sheriff, that fucking little prick, didn't even see it," he shouted in anger.

"What?" Chris asked again.

Thomas looked at him sideways and scratched his head, "You sound like a bad recording, Chris."

Chris wanted to say a few sweet words, but Mackinnon put his hand on his shoulder and held Chris back.

"What, Mr. Nelson? What did the sheriff fail to see?"

"All those accidents and misfortunes," Nelson replied with broad gestures.

Beer slushed out of the bottle, and that stopped him. Thomas preferred to have the beer in his gut, not on the wooden floor of the veranda.

"I put two and two together," Thomas told them. "Someone upset Lorna, and soon enough, something happened. Now, I couldn't see Lorna doing things by herself. She wouldn't dirty her hands, you see. That meant that someone else was involved. Lorna gave money to someone to do those things."

"Were you at the Carters' house last night?" Mackinnon asked him.

Thomas merely nodded and brought the bottle to his mouth again. Then he noticed that he had drunk all the beer in the bottle. He peered inside, and sure enough, there wasn't any left. With a disgusted grimace, Thomas threw the bottle away and took another one.

"What did you see, and what did you do?" Mackinnon asked.

The man shrugged. Then Thomas opened the bottle, and at the same time, he said, "I saw enough, but I did nothing."

"Care to expand on that?" the agent invited him, eyeing the bottle in the man's hand with displeasure.

Thomas caught his glance and said, "Don't worry. I can hold my liquor. Just ask the deputy here," his chin pointed to Chris.

"All right," Mackinnon said. "What did you see?"

"I'll tell you, but you won't like it," Thomas said, shaking his head.

"Care to expend on that?" the agent invited him, eyeing the bottle in the man's hand with displeasure.

Thomas caught his glance and said, "Don't worry, I can hold my liquor. Just ask the deputy here," his chin pointed to Chris.

"All right," Mackinnon said, "what did you see?"

"I'll tell you but you won't like it," Thomas said, shaking his head.

CHAPTER 15 – FATIGUE, DARN EVIDENCE AND NORMA JEAN – EXPLOSIVE COMBINATION

The sheriff's office was quiet at midnight. No one was there to handle the phone or receive any complaints if anything occurred. Chris was the only deputy left on the sheriff's office payroll, and Norma Jean worked only specific shifts.

Both Chris and Mackinnon were the only people still present in the conference room.

Mackinnon had already sent the others back to the motel to catch some shut-eye before eight a.m. when they were supposed to gather in the musty conference room again.

It was late, so Mackinnon hadn't asked many questions about the agents' findings during their interviews and hadn't revealed what he and Chris had discovered.

175

Mackinnon had already called the forensic experts back at the headquarters to request some tests. He needed some concrete proof before going further with the investigation and making an arrest.

Chris yawned loudly. He had tried hard to stifle it, but that was beyond his abilities at that hour. Chris apologized to the agent, and Mackinnon burst into laughter.

"Be serious, Chris, we're both tired. I am so tired that I can't even yawn. We should go to bed. By the way, who's taking care of things in the sheriff's office at night?" he asked and looked curious around.

"Right now? Probably, me," Chris replied and shrugged.

"That's impossible," the agent said. "You can't work day and night."

Chris brushed his fingers over his scalp and ruffled his hair. His skin felt taut and hurt. He squeezed his eyes, and in an attempt to remove the sand lodged in his eyeballs, he rubbed them.

Then, he answered to the agent. "We had another deputy, a guy who worked the graveyard shift, but the sheriff fired him."

"Why?" Mackinnon inquired with curiosity, although he was almost sure he could guess the answer.

"Lorna, why else?" Chris replied in a wearied voice.

"But I don't see how you can work day and night. When did he fire that man?"

"A couple of weeks ago," Chris answered with his characteristic shrug. "I have a cot, there, in the back," he pointed his thumb to the back of the station where the few jail cells were. "I catch some shut-eye during the night anyway, as a norm. It's quiet around here," he observed. "All right, it hasn't been so quiet during the last couple of days, but usually it is."

"All right, then. Go to your cot now, and I'll see you in the morning," Mackinnon threw over his shoulder, and with heavy steps, he let himself out the station.

Chris locked the door behind him and went to take a shower before going to bed. Every fiber in his body screamed in mutiny, and if he was still standing, it was just because of sheer will.

Chris's morning started with a mug of hot coffee. He glanced at his watch. Norma Jean was supposed to arrive in fifteen minutes, and he was happy to have some peace. The woman would chatter like a magpie first thing in the morning and drive him crazy. After so little sleep, his brain was still asleep.

Another cup of coffee would do the trick, he hoped. Chris needed all his faculties around that woman.

Last month, always in the morning like now, Norma Jean tricked him into promising to take her to the fair held in a field near the next town. Chris hadn't been through his first cup at the time, and his brain was muddled. Yet, as he always kept his promises, Chris went with her.

He reckoned that he had had fun. Well, most of the time. There had been a few moments there when he would have liked to put his fingers around Norma Jean's neck and squeeze the life out of her. She wouldn't have been Norma Jean if she had been biddable and charming all the time, Chris grimaced.

When he glanced down the street, Chris saw Norma Jean stroll to the station, as if she had all the time in the world to get there. He groaned loudly and peeked into his cup. With a huge gulp, he drained the rest of the coffee and rushed inside to fix another one.

By the time Norma Jean came in, Chris had already drunk half of the new cup he had fixed for himself and felt fortified enough to deal with her.

Norma Jean slammed the door and threw her hair off her shoulder when she noticed Chris. She watched him suspiciously and didn't bother to greet him.

"What are you hiding?" she inquired with suspicion.

"Hiding?" Chris asked back with surprise.

"Yep, you have that face," Norma Jean fluttered her hand before his eyes.

"That face?" Chris asked again and felt stupid.

"Playing dumb now?" she frowned. "Suit yourself," Norma Jean shrugged and brushed by him. "I suppose you'll want me to make more coffee for your new play friends," she remarked while she put her bag in the top drawer of her desk.

"Play friends?" he frowned.

Norma Jean straightened and sighed. She braced her hands on her hips and replied with resignation, "Yes, I see that I need to make more coffee. This morning, you're so dumb that you could throw yourself on the ground and miss," she shook her head with sadness.

"We can't have that. You might not be the sharpest tool in the shed, but I can't have those nasty *special agents* laughing at you," Norma Jean said and busied herself with the coffee maker under Chris's shocked eyes.

After she turned the coffee maker on, Norma Jean started rummaging for something in one of the lower drawers of the cabinet behind her desk, a pretty curvy part of her body in the air.

Chris's gaze zeroed automatically on the woman's behind, and he couldn't take his eyes from there. The temptation went beyond his usual restraint.

Chris swallowed hard, and his fingers itched. He still argued with himself, not knowing if he should risk it and touch Norma Jean when the agents arrived at the station, talking a storm.

The chatter ceased when they noticed the direction of Chris's gaze, and they stopped shortly inside the station. Their eyes bobbed from Chris's face to the anatomic part that Norma Jean still held in the air.

Chris turned crimson. He didn't know how to explain his lewd behavior.

As if she felt that something had happened, Norma Jean straightened. She glanced at the agents first and then at Chris.

The agents' grins and Chris's scarlet face helped her deduce what had happened, and her narrow eyes aimed at the deputy's face. Then, Norma Jean hissed, "You, leech."

Chris didn't have an excuse at the ready and chose the easy way out. "We'll be in the conference room, Norma Jean," he said with a confidence that he was far from feeling. "When the coffee is ready, you can holler for me to come and get it if you are busy and can't bring it in," Chris continued, trying to keep his voice even. At the same time, he averted his eyes and stared at the wall behind her.

Norma Jean didn't answer but kept her narrowed eyes on him. Chris turned away and invited the agents to follow him to the conference room. Only after he closed the door behind them, Chris breathed deeply with relief.

The agents sat around the table. David would have liked to egg the deputy on, but Mackinnon's unnerving look on him made him keep himself in check.

"I called Gus Carter before we arrived here. I asked him and Edward to come to the station for an interview. They should be here in about five minutes," Mackinnon informed Chris after he consulted his watch.

The deputy nodded and sat down, as well.

"Let's see what you have to say, and then we'll tell you what we discovered last evening," Mackinnon invited the agents to speak.

"We've already organized everything here," Kate said and tapped on her notepad.

"As far as we can see, the only one without an iron-clad alibi is Jeremiah Hicks. He says that he spent the entire weekend with some pals in the next county and came back Sunday night."

The other agents nodded.

"Hicks said that he hadn't seen anyone on the road, and he didn't think that someone could vouch for him, but he'd gotten back to town at midnight," Kate also said to Mackinnon.

Bob cleared his throat, and everyone turned to him. He fidgeted in his seat for a few seconds and then said, "Hum, I have a theory."

Mackinnon nodded and encouraged Bob to talk. He always invited the agent to express his opinions and was delighted when Bob took the initiative. It was a rare event, and Mackinnon hoped that Bob would open more and share his ideas with the others in time.

"What if they all did it?"

Confused eyes zeroed on the agent, and a few brows rose.

"What do you mean?" Chris asked, cursing his foggy brain that morning.

"The town people planned the kill and alibied each other," Bob expanded his explanation and waved his hand with impatience.

It's crystal clear, and they can't see it, Bob thought and had the impulse to knock his head on the top of the table.

"Like those people in Orient Express," he continued, looking from one to the other. Bob was somewhat disappointed to see that no one understood his reference.

Suddenly, Chris slapped his forehead. "I know, Agatha Christie. That murder on the train," he exclaimed, and Bob nodded, satisfied that at least one of them had an inkling of what he was saying.

Mackinnon stared Bob down and asked, "Seriously? That's what you think?"

Bob looked back at Mackinnon mutinously. He was furious. He had just breached his silence policy and spoken, only to be dressed down.

"Don't look at me like that," Mackinnon snapped. "Your idea does have merit, Bob, and I would have considered it in a jiffy if I hadn't thought that the murderer was someone else and with good reason. Chris and I think that Thomas Nelson saw the killer the other night."

"And that person's got a serious motive for both murders," Chris added.

Bob shrugged. He didn't believe them.

"No, really. That's why we invited Gus here," Mackinnon said. "We need to ask Gus a few supplementary questions. And that doesn't mean that you shouldn't present your opinions more often, Bob."

"Maybe Norma Jean will bring that coffee before Gus arrives," David observed. "I could drink a cup or two," he added, and the agents nodded.

Chris stood and stomped to the door. He opened it with a brusque gesture and hollered, "Hey, Norma Jean, how's that coffee coming?"

He turned to the agents and explained, "I don't see her at her desk."

Precisely at that moment, Norma Jean's voice replied in a near shout, "Hold your breeches, Chris. I'll make another pot now."

Chris looked out the door again and saw Norma Jean coming from the sheriff's office with the carafe almost empty.

"What the heck, Norma Jean? Where did the coffee go?" Chris snapped at her and braced his hands on his hips.

"The sheriff," Norma Jean pointed to the sheriff's office with the top of her head. "He's got guests," she shrugged. "You didn't think I'd tell him that this coffee was for you, did you?" she asked with irony in her voice.

He shook his head with resignation.

"I'll make another pot of coffee now, don't worry. Just a few more minutes, all right?" Norma Jean replied, and her pleasant attitude confused Chris.

Norma Jean noticed his confusion and guessed what had triggered it. She loved it when she could cloud Chris's mind, so she smiled widely at him, showing two rows of pearly little teeth.

He shook his head and merely turned back to the conference room. He closed the door behind him with care, and then, he sighed deeply and headed to the table.

He felt the inquiring eyes focused on him and clarified, "Just a minor setback. Norma Jean is making another pot for us right now."

Chris had scarcely sat down when someone knocked on the door. *Impossible, she couldn't have done it yet*, he thought.

Mackinnon said, "Come in."

The door opened and allowed Gus and Edward Carter to get into the room.

"That woman," Gus said tartly, pointing his thumb in Norma Jean's general direction, "the one with the big mouth and red hair, Norma Jean, that's her name, she said we should just come in."

Gus seemed pretty riled about the young woman's behavior. Chris guessed that he wasn't just upset about what happened Sunday night. He was sure that Norma Jean had had something to say to Gus that morning, as well.

Edward kept silent. He stood close to his father, and his eyes danced from one agent to the other with curiosity.

Mackinnon noticed that the boy had taken after his mother. His hair, eyes, and shape of the face showed his parentage as clearly as any DNA test. Gus's contribution lay in the boy's height and propensity for good food. Although on the brink of his eighteenth year of life, Edward already carried a healthy gut.

"Have a seat," Mackinnon indicated to the chairs that he had brought to the table that morning.

Gus sat immediately with a contented sigh. Edward seemed to balk at first, but then he followed his father's example. His face showed no emotion.

"I called you here this morning because we have some questions for Edward," the agent began, and his words startled Gus.

"What kind of questions? The kid wasn't at home that evening," Gus rushed to explain. "Normally, Lorna wouldn't have let him spend the night out of the house on a Sunday evening. However, the boy took what he could. Didn't you, boy?" Gus asked his son and then whacked Edward over the back heartily.

The young man winced, and not only because of the whacking. Edward was sick of his father's calling him *the boy.*

"Yes, you told us that Edward wasn't at home that evening," Mackinnon agreed. "Yet, he left the house earlier, came back when you were away, and then left again," he explained to Gus. "Isn't that the truth, Edward?" Mackinnon asked, and Gus's mouth fell and hung open.

Edward didn't answer. He just stared at Mackinnon with unreadable eyes.

Gus recovered from his surprise soon enough and nudged Edward, "Tell them that they're wrong, son."

"You're wrong," Edward dutifully repeated his father's words.

Mackinnon studied him carefully and then replied, "People saw you..." He waited a moment to see if Edward would say something. When he noticed that the young man kept stubbornly silent, he continued, "And not only one person."

Edward just shrugged with indifference as if the agent hadn't talked about him. Gus's face turned grey under the implications conveyed in the agent's words. He wanted to slap his son silly and make him deny the allegations.

"And not only at home, but at the motel as well," Mackinnon delivered the final blow.

Yet, the result wasn't the one he expected. That very moment the door opened, and a talkative Norma Jean entered, carrying the coffee, and surprisingly, some cookies.

"Now, the coffee's ready. I don't know about you, but I'm pretty sure that Chris hasn't had a bite today, so I ran across the street and brought something to snack on," the woman advanced into the room, talking gaily. Norma Jean didn't wait for any reply.

Edward sprung off his chair and grabbed the woman. She squealed and dropped the coffee and the cookies on the floor. He pulled Norma Jean up, and her feet left the floor. She flailed her arms and legs, trying to kick him. Sick of her attempts to hurt him, Edward retrieved a switchblade from his pant pocket and put it at her neck. Norma Jean froze instantly, and her eyes filled with tears.

Gus grasped his chest and started panting.

Mackinnon stood slowly and said, "Edward, you have nowhere to go. Don't make it worse. Just let the woman go."

The young man looked at him, both with hatred and fear. His eyes exposed the cornered animal that laid beneath the surface.

Kate slowly went to Gus. She was afraid that the older man had a heart attack. Edward monitored her moves with sharp eyes and squeezed Norma Jean harder. She whimpered and gazed pleadingly at Chris.

Chris didn't show any visible emotion to what was happening. He was focused on Edward's movements and avoided Norma Jean's begging eyes thoroughly.

After a few moments, an ugly grin flourished on Edward's lips, and the hand with the knife relaxed somewhat. The young man reckoned that he had won that round, although he didn't have a definite idea about what he would do next.

The moment the hand with the knife relaxed, Chris was on top of him. The deputy wrung Edward's arm violently, and the blade moved from Norma Jean's neck.

With one hand, Chris snatched Norma Jean from Edward's clutches and pushed her aside. His fist made brutal contact with the young man's nose and broke it. Edward fell on the ground with a resonant thump. When the bone snapped, a terrible sound filled the suddenly quiet room and made the agents wince. Blood spewed and blinded Edward, who was shouting in pain now. He tried to stop the blood with his sound hand but didn't succeed.

Chris looked like he wished to punch Edward once more, but Mackinnon stopped him, putting his hand on Chris's arm. Then, he said in a severe tone of voice, "I think that's enough, Chris. Let the boy go."

Chris looked up at Mackinnon with weary eyes. He seemed ready to ignore the order but then pushed Edward away and stood up. Chris turned to Norma Jean, who had remained where he had thrown her earlier, and he helped her stand.

"Are you all right?" Chris asked her softly, brushing a curl of hair behind her ear.

Her eyes round and full of awe, Norma Jean nodded. She stared at Chris with something akin to admiration.

Chris noticed that tears clung to the woman's lashes and ran down on her cheeks, so he wiped them with his thumbs. He pulled the woman into his arms carefully, and Norma Jean glued to Chris's body like a fern.

None of them paid attention to Edward's howl of pain. Mackinnon had already popped his joint back and fastened the handcuffs on him. He pulled the boy up, and then he noticed the agents' behavior. Mesmerized, his agents were staring in Chris's direction. Mackinnon looked around Bob, and for a moment, seeing Chris holding Norma Jean in his arms, shocked him.

Unexpectedly, the door was thrown open and slammed into the wall. Everyone but Chris and Norma Jean turned to the door. The sheriff was standing there with a gun in his hand.

Mackinnon lifted an eyebrow, looking pointedly at the gun. The sheriff blushed but didn't lower his weapon.

"What the heck is going on around here?" Ken asked, and his eyes fell on Norma Jean and Chris. "What the heck did you do to Norma Jean, Chris? I'll have your head, you son of a bitch," the sheriff shouted from the top of his lungs.

It seemed that Norma Jean needed only that to recover. She disengaged herself from Chris's embrace but kept one hand on his chest possessively, which made the female agents muse. The man wouldn't have many days as a bachelor left. They were sure Norma Jean would snatch him in no time, and Chris wouldn't even know what hit him.

"You're two bricks short of a full load, Ken. Chris saved my life, you, idiot," she scolded him. "Where the heck, were you when I had a knife at my throat?" she ended in a full shout.

The sheriff stared at her as if she had grown horns on her forehead. He wasn't able to articulate a sound for a few moments.

"Who put a knife to your neck?" he finally managed to ask.

"That prick there," she pointed to Edward. "If it hadn't been for Chris, here, Lord knows what would have happened to me," she replied belligerently.

CHAPTER 16 – TYING LOOSE ENDS

The sheriff wiped his forehead. The heat was oppressive for November, even though it was still early morning. Ken replaced his weapon in his holster, and then he borrowed the closest chair and sat down. The events were too much for his understanding, and Ken felt overwhelmed.

"Does anyone care to tell me what's going on?" the sheriff asked. Ken was sick of being left in the dark all the time.

"I think that the boy should be telling the story. What do you think, Edward?" Mackinnon asked.

Chris kept his hard eyes trained on the young man, and Edward shook in his boots. Chris's appearance and demeanor were far from what Edward had seen before, and he couldn't deal with that new Chris.

"No, my boy won't say a word," Gus intervened. He came behind Edward and put a hand on his son's shoulder. Then, he stared Mackinnon down. "I'll call my lawyer first," Gus continued. "Will you arrest him now, or can I take him home?"

"You won't take him home," Chris went off like a rocket. He helped Norma Jean sit in his chair and came near Edward, ready to snatch him and put him in prison.

"Are you out of your fricking mind?" the sheriff bellowed. "Are you messing with Gus Carter? You're history, Henderson. Do you hear me?"

"Shut your mouth, Ken, or I will shut it for you myself," Norma Jean jumped into the fray, and the agents had to hide their smiles. "Chris knows what he's doing. Now, I can't say the same thing about you, can I? If your brains were dynamite, you couldn't blow your nose," she added, and Ken turned scarlet.

"What the heck are you talking about, woman?"

Norma Jean shook her head as if she were at a loss for words. "Someone enlightens him before I lose my temper and take care of his ugly mug," she said and started to the door. "I'll bring some coffee, sandwiches, and cookies from across the street, Chris," she turned and said to the deputy.

When he raised his eyebrow inquiringly, Norma Jean waved her hand nonchalantly and added, "For everyone, yes, don't twist your breeches in a knot now." She waltzed out of the room, and a satisfied smile suddenly claimed Chris's lips.

"Are you sure you can handle her, Henderson?" David inquired ironically but shut up as soon as Mackinnon glanced at him.

"Don't overtax your brain, David, with what I can or cannot do," Chris replied with indifference. "So, Mackinnon, what about the little prick?" he asked, pointing to Edward.

"Read him his rights, print him, and lock him," the agent replied drily. "Don't forget to call a doctor to see him, although, in my opinion, he's just fine."

The sheriff's eyes widened when the agent's words penetrated his brain. Norma Jean's words and attitude had already shocked him, and now, Ken couldn't find his bearings anymore. Things were turning weirder and weirder, and he needed a compass to find his way.

Chris's and Gus's voices seeped into the room. They were quarreling. Gus demanded to let his son go. However, Chris wouldn't have allowed Edward to leave for anything in the world.

"So, will anyone tell me what's going on?" Ken insisted.

"We'll wait for Chris to come back if you don't mind," Mackinnon said. "The deputy was extremely helpful in this investigation, sheriff. He deserves to be here."

Ken Willow shrugged. He didn't care whether Chris was there or not. He just wanted to understand what was going on.

Five minutes later, Chris returned to the room, helping Norma Jean. The woman had come with some coffee, sandwiches, and cakes. The two of them put the food on the table. To everyone's bewilderment, Norma Jean poured the coffee herself and offered sugar and milk to the agents.

When she left the room, everybody attacked the sandwiches.

"Has Gus left, or is he still in the station?" Mackinnon inquired.

"He left to bring the lawyer," Chris replied, unwrapping a ham and cheese sandwich.

He took a healthy bite and sighed. Chris was ravenous. After the events of the morning, he could eat a horse.

"Chris is here now," the sheriff observed with sarcasm and helped himself to one of the sandwiches.

Mackinnon glanced his way and didn't bother to hide his contempt. He took a lazy bite of his sandwich, and only after he chewed, slowly, as slowly as possible, he started talking.

"Lorna Carter had her hitman," he said, and the sheriff scoffed.

"Be serious, man," Ken said, laughing. "Lorna, and a hitman, huh."

Mackinnon looked at him with steely eyes and nodded.

"Yes, sheriff. She had a hitman. We'll give you the report at the end of the investigation, and you'll see how many things you chose not to see for what they were. By the way, OSBI took over Lewis Wilson's case," Mackinnon mentioned. "So that you know."

The sheriff scoffed again. "There's no case. The kid just up and left."

"Yes, he did, like Campbell's daughter, and Hick's attack," David murmured, but the sheriff heard his words and frowned.

"What the heck are you talking about?" Ken shouted.

Chris had had enough. As he had already polished his sandwich off and a couple of cookies, the deputy discovered that he wanted to answer to the sheriff's question.

"The guy in the motel, the one stabbed several times, was Lorna's hitman. We do have serious evidence in some of the cases. For instance, the DNA of Emily Logan's newborn proves that Anderson was the father. Anyway, the idea is that Lorna needed to meet with Anderson on Sunday evening. Only they knew the reason. She sent Gus on a wild goose chase to the mayor's ranch, and she allowed Edward to spend the night with some friends," Chris said and poured some more coffee in his cup.

After adding some sugar and cream, he took a mouthful and then continued.

"However, Edward returned home. Why? We can only guess. Probably, he forgot something," Chris shrugged. "Anyway, Edward got there just in time to hear his mother talk to Anderson. He put two and two together and realized who the man was. He certainly listened to his mother's conversation with the man, and I suppose that then he found out that Anderson had raped Emily. Otherwise, I don't think that Edward would have had a reason to kill Lorna or Anderson."

"This's just speculation," Ken scoffed. "There's no proof that the boy killed anyone. Do you know what Gus will do to us, you, idiot?"

"But we do have proof," Mackinnon retorted. "We spoke to some people who can place Edward Carter at both crime scenes at the time of the murders. The boy's prints are on the knives."

"The knives came from the Carters' kitchen," Ken argued. "Of course, Edward's prints should be on the knives."

"Maybe so," Chris intervened. "However, have you seen the lacerations on Edward's hand?" he asked the sheriff.

Ken didn't reply but glowered at Chris.

"Well, Edward's got lacerations, all right. The forensic experts determined that the blood at the base of both knives didn't belong to the victims. We're confident that the DNA test will prove that it belongs to Edward," Chris concluded.

Ken didn't argue anymore. He recognized the validity of their reasoning and guessed that the forensic evidence would back Chris's conclusion. The man also understood that he didn't have many days left in the position of a sheriff.

EPILOGUE

Norma Jean heard the hammering coming from the other side of the cottage when she stopped her car. A broad smile lightened her face, and she threw her hair back. She had driven with her windows down, and her hair was windblown now.

She stepped out of the car. Then she leaned inside and took a basket covered with a white kitchen towel. Her mouth watered when the aroma of the freshly roasted chicken tickled her nose.

Norma Jean put the basket on the ground near the car and leaned back inside to take the bag with the red wine bottle and the box with cookies she had baked that morning. She also picked up her handbag from the back seat.

Norma Jean closed the car door and collected everything carefully. Then she started to the back of the cottage, where she found Chris. The man was swinging a hammer with dedication.

Chris had finished with the addition of the rooms he had planned, and now, he was building a veranda. It was supposed to go round the entire perimeter of the house and shelter a swinging bench and flowers.

"Hey there," Norma Jean greeted him, and Chris stopped and turned his head to her.

He wiped his brow and smiled when he saw what she was carrying.

"I see you brought food," he chuckled.

"I imagined you'd need some," Norma Jean replied. "Plus, a bottle of wine. We do need to celebrate your election, sheriff," she winked at him.

"Norma Jean, no matter how much you'd try to bribe me, baby, you won't get your position back. I don't feel like shooting myself in the leg," Chris chuckled again.

"You, ass," she yelled at him. She bent and took a twig off the ground and threw it at him. "I'm not trying to bribe you. I've cooked for you all morning, Chris Henderson and..."

Chris pulled Norma Jean into his arms and shut her up with a hard kiss on her lips.

AUTHOR'S BIOGRAPHY

Born in Europe, some time ago, the writer started loving books very early. The next step was easy: writing became a dream and a purpose.

Roxana enjoys writing and baking. These two work very well hand in hand. She also enjoys spending time with her dog - or at least most of the time, as he is a hellion.

One trip to Scotland made her lose her heart to a beautiful country and extraordinary people, and that is why she chose a Scottish detective to promote most of her crime stories.

Books by Roxana Nastase:

Mayhem on Nightingale Street – McNamara Series – Vol I - standalone

Scents and Shadows – McNamara Series – Vol II - standalone

Relative Bounds – McNamara Series – Vol III - standalone

A Suitable Epitaph – MacKay – Canadian Detectives – Vol I – standalone

An Immigrant – MacKay – Canadian Detectives – Vol II – standalone

The Man in the Elevator

Team Building with a Twist

Payback is a Bitch

To hear about future releases, please, subscribe to my newsletter on:

www.roxananastase.weebly.com.

No other type of emails will be sent to you.

www.ingramcontent.com/pod-product-compliance
Lightning Source LLC
Chambersburg PA
CBHW060326260626
47160CB00007B/2696